Nancy Geddy was a real girl who lived in Williamsburg, Virginia, in the 1760s. Her father was a silversmith, goldsmith, and watch repairer. Williamsburg was the capital of the Virginia colony. Beginning in 1765 with their protest over the Stamp Act, people in Williamsburg helped lead the thirteen colonies to independence.

Today, Nancy's house and her family's foundry are part of Colonial Williamsburg, a living history museum. Colonial Williamsburg's Historic Area has been restored to look the way it did at the time of the American Revolution. People in costume tell the story of Virginia's contributions to American independence and show visitors how Williamsburg residents lived during the colonial era.

At Colonial Williamsburg, you can see where Nancy lived and the Geddy Foundry, where her friend Tom Dugar was an apprentice. You can also visit the Benjamin Powell House, and maybe even do a few chores. You can shop at the John Greenhow Store, where Nancy bought the ribbon for her first ball gown with the Christmas coin from her father.

The Colonial Williamsburg Foundation is proud to have worked with Joan Lowery Nixon on the Young Americans series. Staff members met with Mrs. Nixon and identified sources for her research. People at Colonial Williamsburg read each book to make sure it was as accurate as possible, from the way the characters speak to what they eat to the clothes they wear. Mrs. Nixon's note at the end of the book tells exactly what we know about Nancy, her family, and her friends.

Another way to learn more about the life of Nancy Geddy and her family and friends is to experience Williamsburg for yourself. A visit to Colonial Williamsburg is a journey to the past—we invite you to join us on that journey and bring history to life.

Cary Carson

Cary Carson
Vice President—Research
The Colonial Williamsburg Foundation

Nancy's Story
1765

YOUNG AMERICANS

Colonial Williamsburg

Nancy's Story

1765

JOAN LOWERY NIXON

Delacorte Press

Published by
Delacorte Press
an imprint of
Random House Children's Books
a division of Random House, Inc.
1540 Broadway
New York, New York 10036

Visit us on the Web! www.randomhouse.com/kids
Educators and librarians, for a variety of teaching tools, visit us at
www.randomhouse.com/teachers
www.history.org

Library of Congress Cataloging-in-Publication Data
Nixon, Joan Lowery.
  Nancy's story: 1765 / Joan Lowery Nixon.
    p. cm.—(Young Americans ; 3)
  Summary: In 1765, twelve-year-old Nancy worries about the effect of the British
Stamp Act on her father's silversmith business in Williamsburg and about how to
get along with her new stepmother.
  ISBN 0-385-32679-3
  1. Williamsburg (Va.)—History—Colonial period, ca. 1600–1774—Juvenile
fiction. [1. Williamsburg (Va.)—History—Colonial period, ca.1600–1774—
Fiction. 2. Stepmothers—Fiction.] I. Title.

PZ7.N65 Nap 2000
[Fic]—dc21

00-029503

The text of this book is set in 12-point Minion.
Book design by Patrice Sheridan
Manufactured in the United States of America
October 2000
10 9 8 7 6 5 4 3 2 1
BVG

Contents

Prologue

Chip Hahn frowned at Lori Smith as they crossed Nicholson Street in Colonial Williamsburg. "You're wrong," he insisted. "The colonists got mad because the Stamp Act meant they'd have to pay more taxes."

"I'm not wrong. You are," Lori answered. "You just don't get it."

Chip glanced over at one of the booths, where Molly Otts was arranging a display of ribboned caps and cocked hats. "Oh, yeah?" he said, grinning at Lori. "Let's ask Mrs. Otts. She'll tell you I'm right and you're wrong."

"Go ahead. Ask her," Lori said. "Somebody needs to set you straight."

Mrs. Otts smiled as she saw Chip and Lori race toward her.

"Are you here for the story I promised you about Nancy Geddy?" she asked.

"Oh. The story. Sure," Chip said, suddenly remembering why they had come. "Some of the other kids are on their way over, too. But before they get here, would you answer a question for us?"

"If I can," Mrs. Otts said. "What's the question?"

"When the Stamp Act was passed in 1765, didn't the colonists get mad because they had to pay more taxes?"

"You might say so," Mrs. Otts answered.

Chip smirked at Lori. "See? I was right," he said.

"But that was just part of it," Mrs. Otts continued. "'Tis true that the colonists didn't enjoy paying taxes, but they were sensible people and realized that some taxes were necessary.

"As good Englishmen," she added, "they strongly believed that only the House of Burgesses—whose representatives they had elected—should tax Virginians."

"See! You weren't right, Chip! I was!" Lori crowed.

Mrs. Otts sighed. "It took courage to stand up for what they believed, and they suffered for it. When the colonists rebelled, tax stamp agents throughout

2

the colonies resigned, so no stamps were available in many of the colonies, including Virginia. The stamps showed that the taxes on an official document, such as a contract or license, had been paid. Without a stamp, a document was not legal. And without legal documents, the courts were closed and government business could not be conducted."

Mrs. Otts laid a row of ruffled caps on the table in front of her, smoothing their ribbons. "The Stamp Act caused a great concern for Nancy Geddy's father and thus for his family. When the act was signed in 1765, Nancy Geddy was twelve years old, mature enough to see what harm could come to her father's silversmith business. This certainly added to Nancy's troubles."

"What troubles?" Chip asked.

"Please wait before you tell us, Mrs. Otts," Lori interrupted. She waved frantically to Keisha and Stewart and her other classmates, who were approaching Market Square. "Here come some of the other kids from our class. They'll want to hear the story, too."

Their friends raced each other to the booth. When they arrived, Lori nodded. "Now you can tell us," she said.

"Tell us what?" Stewart asked.

"The story," Lori said. "About Nancy Geddy."

"The market's not officially open yet, so we'll have time," Mrs. Otts said. "Now, let's see. Where shall I begin?"

"You said something about Nancy's troubles," Chip reminded her.

"Ah, yes. Nancy Geddy thought her troubles began when her father, James Geddy, Jr., remarried."

"You told us about *John* Geddy in your story about Ann McKenzie," Keisha said. "Was James related to John?"

"James was John's elder brother," Mrs. Otts answered. "John was Nancy's uncle. James and John had been trained to be silversmiths, but their two elder brothers—David and William—operated the Geddy Foundry."

"We visited the foundry," Stewart said. "The interpreter told us that James Geddy once lived on the property."

"He did. James was the third son, but it was he, not his elder brothers, who bought the property, which included the foundry, from his mother."

"Did James Geddy work in the foundry?" Keisha asked.

"I'm sure some of his work as a silversmith and

4

watchmaker was done at the foundry, but he owned and operated a shop on the property as well. James rented the foundry to David and William. The foundry and James's shop were separate businesses."

Mrs. Otts smiled and said, "Now, let me tell you about Nancy. Her mother had died when Nancy was but an infant, and for much of her childhood, Nancy's grandmother lived with her and her father.

"Grandmother Anne Geddy did all the things Nancy's mother would have done—managed the household and taught Nancy reading, writing, ciphering, and housewifery. As Nancy grew older her grandmother let her begin taking on many of the household chores. Then, when Nancy was ten, her father brought home his new wife."

Keisha looked at Lori. "Uh-oh," Keisha said. "*A stepmother.* This isn't going to be a Cinderella kind of story, is it?"

"No, indeed," Mrs. Otts said. "Nancy's stepmother tried to be fair. It's just that she didn't seem to understand growing girls. And, in turn, Nancy didn't try very hard to understand her."

Mrs. Otts stepped out of the booth and gestured

toward the grass. "Sit down and make yourselves comfortable. I'm going to tell you about Nancy, who was twelve years old in 1765, and how she . . . Well, you'll see. You may be surprised how Nancy's life isn't all that different from your own."

Chapter One

Nancy Geddy, clutching her market basket, stomped on the dried leaves in her path. She angrily kicked at a small stone, sending it flying. "Why does she always have to interfere?" Nancy muttered under her breath.

Grace, the family's house slave, a tall girl only a few years older than Nancy, spoke up from behind Nancy. "Sorry, Miss Nancy," Grace said. "I didn't exactly hear what you said."

"Never mind, Grace. 'Twas nothing," Nancy answered. Although the day—Wednesday, October 30, 1765—was crisp, sunny, and beautiful, Nancy scowled at a nearby squirrel that was scampering up the trunk of an oak tree.

She was certain that Grace had heard her. But

Grace, who wanted no part of any problem—no matter what the problem was—offered only one infuriating answer to anything Nancy complained about: "You must make do, Miss Nancy. Just make do."

But Nancy didn't want to make do.

For three years—ever since she was nine—Nancy had walked to Market Square each morning, first accompanied by her grandmother, who had lived with Nancy and her father, and then by Grace. Nancy had loved those mornings with her grandmother and had eagerly learned how to buy meats and vegetables with care. She felt special pride when, a few months later, Grandmother entrusted her with the task of doing the daily marketing.

On one occasion at Market Square, Nancy had met Mrs. Anne Wetherburn, a family friend. Mrs. Wetherburn had patted Nancy's shoulder and beamed at her. "Your housewifery skills are a credit to your grandmother," she'd said. "You're so like your dear mother, Nancy. I know how proud of you your father must be and how proud your mother would have been."

Nancy had happily smiled in return. She'd been certain that the daily chore of marketing, in addition to her other household tasks, was what her mother would have wanted her to do. Nancy basked in her grandmother's praise, too. Anne Geddy was delighted with Nancy's growing ability to care for the family and their beautiful two-story house at the corner of Palace and Duke of Gloucester streets.

Working side by side with Grace, who had only recently joined the household, Nancy had absorbed Grandmother's lessons on how to do the chores of laundry, gardening, plain sewing, raising poultry, pickling or potting food to preserve it, cooking the meals, airing the mattresses, dusting, and sweeping the floors with wet sand, following with a sweeping of fresh sage.

There were also special lessons just for Nancy. She'd learned to plan meals for her father, her grandmother, herself, and Grace, and she'd learned to grow her own vegetables and herbs.

Nancy also enjoyed her grandmother's lessons in reading, writing, and ciphering. Anne Geddy always had plenty of hugs for her and liked to tell Nancy affectionate stories about her mother or about Nancy's baby years.

Nancy sighed as she thought about her mother. She had died when Nancy was still an infant. Nancy's father had once told her that her mother possessed a joyful spirit. She had smiled and laughed easily and had doted on her baby daughter.

"Dear child, you have your mother's lovely features," he had said. "I see the same soft brown hair and sparkling eyes." He had smiled. "And the exact same saucy tilt to your nose."

Only a baby when she lost her mother, Nancy was too young to have memories and couldn't even picture her mother's face. But sometimes she'd whisper over and over, "Elizabeth . . . Elizabeth." It was a lovely name. It was her mother's name.

And often—especially during quiet dinners and long evenings when Grandmother had retired early and Papa seemed to be lost inside himself—Nancy wished with all her heart that she could have her mother back again.

Beautiful, loving Elizabeth would hug Nancy, and sing to her, and read with her, and teach her to bake tarts even juicier and sweeter than Mrs. Wetherburn's. And oh, how they would laugh together!

Then fate had played a cruel trick. When Nancy was ten an Elizabeth *had* come into her life. The problem was that it was the wrong Elizabeth.

Elizabeth Waddill was quiet, solemn, and plainspoken. She wasn't given to laughter, comforting hugs, or loving pats. Worst of all, she was Nancy's stepmother, and when she moved into the Geddys' home, Grandmother moved to her own property several miles away.

James Geddy had brought Elizabeth home and informed Nancy they were to be married. At first, shock had kept Nancy from speaking out. She knew Miss Waddill, the plain, shy, unmarried sister of William Waddill. William was an engraver who had occasionally worked with Nancy's father.

Common courtesy had caused Nancy to hold her tongue until Elizabeth had left the room and couldn't hear them. It was then Nancy had confronted her father in tears.

"How could you decide to marry Miss Waddill without telling me?" she had cried.

James Geddy's face had reddened and he had stared down at his boot tops. "A man needs a wife to manage his household, and a daughter needs a mother."

"She's *not* a mother! She's a *step*mother!" Nancy had sobbed. She knew that her father hated confrontations of any sort, but she was too upset to care. "And she wasn't friendly to me. Couldn't you see? She didn't even smile."

"She's shy. And she's a little concerned about being mother to a half-grown daughter. You'll find when you know Elizabeth that—"

"Elizabeth!" Nancy had shouted. "Why does her name have to be Elizabeth?"

Nancy had wanted her father to hold her in his arms, to reassure her that he loved her and that he had always appreciated all she'd done to help create a happy home for him. But he'd sunk into a nearby chair and dropped his chin to his chest. "Nancy, your outburst surprises me. I'd expected you to be joyful about my marriage. I thought you would do your best to make your new mother feel welcome."

Nancy knew her father was right. Fighting to bring her tears under control, she'd said, "I beg your pardon, Papa."

Mr. Geddy had nodded, but his eyes were still filled with disappointment. "Elizabeth will be a good wife to me and a good mother to you, child. I hope you understand that you and I have said all that needs to be said about the matter. We'll speak no more about it. When Elizabeth returns, please greet her with a pleasant expression on your face and address her as Mama."

Nancy had shuddered. "Must I, Papa? I have never called anyone Mama."

Mr. Geddy had rested a hand on Nancy's shoulder and looked at her beseechingly. "Then this would be a good time to begin. Would it not?"

Grandmother had called Nancy to the kitchen. She'd held Nancy's hand and spoken softly. "When your grandfather died I chose not to marry again. However, there were many times that I missed him keenly." She sighed and continued. "Your father and mother were very happy together. I can well understand why he would want to experience that kind of happiness again."

"I make Papa happy," Nancy said stubbornly.

"Yes, you do, but happiness between two married adults is the type of happiness that a daughter cannot provide, not even one who is dearly loved."

"She will want to manage everything," Nancy protested.

"As she should," Grandmother said. "Although you have learned much about managing your father's household, there is still much more for you to learn." She pulled a handkerchief from the pocket inside her skirt and handed it to Nancy. "Dry your eyes, dear. Let's do our best to make Elizabeth feel welcome."

When Nancy and Grandmother rejoined Papa, Elizabeth was with him. Nancy had curtseyed. She had kept her voice soft and gentle and forced a pleasant expression to her face. "Welcome to our family, Mama," she had said.

Mr. Geddy's face had flushed with pleasure, and

Grandmother had nodded her approval, but Elizabeth had solemnly looked into Nancy's eyes and murmured, "Thank you, child."

At that moment Nancy had realized that Elizabeth had silently taken charge.

Nancy had been right. In the days, weeks, and months that followed the wedding, Elizabeth hadn't tried to understand Grandmother's and Nancy's arrangements for the household. She had quietly and firmly made changes, sometimes criticizing the way things had been done, and organized everything her own way. To add to Nancy's resentment, her father—busy with his work as silversmith and watchmaker—had seemed perfectly content with whatever Elizabeth had wanted to do.

Then, to make everything even worse, Elizabeth announced she was having a child, and the household was subdued for nearly nine months as she went through a miserably ill confinement.

At last she had given birth to a healthy, husky baby boy, who was christened James Geddy III. There had been happy chatter among friends and neighbors about the Geddys' good fortune of having a boy to carry on James Geddy's name—as if Nancy, being a girl, didn't count.

"Mistress Nancy?"

Suddenly Grace's voice broke into Nancy's thoughts.

"What is it, Grace?" Nancy said.

"Mistress Nancy, I told you Mistress Cripps has got some fine young pullets over there," Grace answered.

Nancy grimaced. "I would like to buy some pullets," she said. "They would make a good dinner for Papa. But I've been instructed to bring home a leg of mutton."

"Mutton's good, too," Grace quickly said.

"Oh, bother, Grace! You know mutton isn't as delicious as young hens, basted with butter sauce and roasted. If Elizabeth would just allow me to sprig the mutton through and through with rosemary, as in one of my mother's receipts, it could be tasty. But instead she roasts it *her* way, with not so much as a pinch of salt to keep the meat from tasting strong."

Grace, looking uncomfortable, took a step backward. "Mistress Nancy, if you'll buy the apples Mistress Geddy asked for, I'll take them right back to her. She's been so sick with the baby she's expectin' next spring, I'd feel easier if someone was with her and little Jamie. He can be a handful."

Nancy nodded, remembering how sixteen-month-old Jamie just that morning had pulled

15

everything out of her chest of drawers, scattering the contents around her bedchamber. Even though she loved her little brother, she often wished that Elizabeth were more interested in correcting *his* behavior than in correcting hers.

"Your mother—" Grace began.

"*Step*mother," Nancy interrupted.

Grace nodded. "Your stepmother, she don't look well. I know lots of women find the early months hard, but she's so ill, sometimes I fear for her."

"She complained of being ill the whole time she was carrying Jamie," Nancy grumbled. Before she could stop herself from saying what she thought, she added, "I think she likes to rest and let other people do her work."

"Now, Mistress Nancy, be fair," Grace chided.

Nancy quickly reached into her pocket, pulled out some coins, and handed them to Grace. "You're right, Grace, and I thank you for thinking of Mistress Geddy's welfare. Please buy the apples at Mr. Potter's stall and return home. I can do the rest of the marketing by myself."

Grace hesitated. "You don't 'spect to need me?"

Of course I'll need you, Nancy thought impatiently, *but what does it matter when Elizabeth seems to need you even more?* She shook her head. "Hurry home,

Grace," she answered, trying to soften her order with a smile.

Grace was three years older and at least five inches taller, yet at times Nancy felt many years older than the other girl. Maybe it was because Grace only had to do what she was told and didn't have the responsibility of pleasing a father, placating a stepmother, and often being the only one to take charge of an active little brother.

As Nancy began to purchase the items Elizabeth had listed, the basket grew heavier and heavier. Nancy, feeling out of sorts, wished she had Grace with her to help carry the many items. Grace *should* be with her. Grace always had been with her. But no longer. Elizabeth had changed everything.

Not watching where she was going, Nancy hurried around one of the stalls and nearly collided with a blond girl who was Nancy's exact height.

"Hannah!" Nancy cried to her best friend. "I beg your pardon. I wasn't watching where I was going."

"Neither was I," Hannah said with a grin. "I was busy searching the crowd for you."

Hannah's plump, rosy-cheeked mother, Annabelle Powell, came over with her other daughter, Ann. "All that happy giggling means that you've found Nancy," Mrs. Powell said to Hannah.

She held out a twist of paper to Nancy, Hannah, and Ann. "Have a candied orange peel," she said. "And I'll enjoy one, too. Sweets to the sweet, I say." She waited until they had chosen orange peels, then popped another one into her own mouth.

Nancy licked the sugar from her lips. "I love candied orange peels," she said.

"Time will soon be taken up with the twelve days of Christmas, with all its balls, weddings, and parties," Mrs. Powell said to Nancy. "While we can, why don't we have a cooking lesson? It will be good for you, Hannah, and Ann to learn to make mince pies and custards. Suppose we have a cooking lesson tomorrow morning? Would you like that?"

"Oh, yes! Thank you, Mrs. Powell!" Nancy gave a little jump of excitement. What could be more fun than being with her best friend in the Powells' warm, cozy kitchen, baking good things to eat?

"Good," Mrs. Powell said. "Do you think your mother would like to join us?"

"I'm certain she would not," Nancy answered quickly. "She hasn't been feeling well."

"I'm sorry," Mrs. Powell said, "but at least we'll see you tomorrow, Nancy. Ten o'clock."

"Ten o'clock," Nancy echoed. "I'll be there."

Her bad feelings quickly disappeared as she resumed her shopping with the Powell family. She laughed at Mrs. Powell's and Hannah's happy chatter, rejoicing in their friendship. Nothing could spoil this wonderful day.

Chapter Two

When Nancy arrived home, she carried her purchases to the kitchen, where Grace was boiling water for spearmint tea. Grace gave a nod toward the house. "The tea seems to settle the mistress's stomach," she said.

"How is she?" Nancy asked.

"She don't feel any better," Grace answered.

As Nancy wiped off the leg of mutton with a damp cloth, preparing it for the roasting spit, Grace took the onions and potatoes from the basket and placed them on a nearby shelf.

"I met Hannah and her mother at Market Square," Nancy told Grace. "And Mrs. Powell told me the funniest story. Her cousin came to visit and brought along her new pup. It barked at Cyclops, their cat, which terrified him. To get away from the pup, Cyclops leaped to the highest spot around—Mr. Powell's head—and dug his claws into Mr. Powell's wig. The wig flew off—Cyclops, too."

As Grace and Nancy laughed at the story, Elizabeth, carrying a squirming Jamie, stepped into the kitchen. She looked weary and pale, and her voice was tired. "Nancy," she said, "you seem to have nothing to do at the present. Will you please watch Jamie for me? I have mending that must be done, and it's hard to keep Jamie out of the mending basket."

"I was only telling Grace that—"

"If you please," Elizabeth repeated firmly. Without another word she thrust Jamie at Nancy and left the kitchen.

Nancy snuggled with Jamie, nuzzling his soft brown curls. "You might as well be mine," she grumbled. "I seem to be the one who cares for you the most."

Grace smiled as she slowly shook her head. "Mistress Nancy, you know a little boy Jamie's age takes lots of watchin' by everybody who can do the job. And your mother—"

"*Step*mother!"

"Your stepmother sometimes seems too ill to care for Jamie."

21

Nancy had her own opinion about Elizabeth's so-called illness, and there was no point in sharing it with Grace. She tied a cloak over Jamie's gown and put on her own cloak. Still irritated with Elizabeth, Nancy needed a friend with whom she could talk—a good friend like Tom.

Thomas Dugar, a tall, tanned fourteen-year-old with blue eyes and pale blond hair, served as an apprentice to Nancy's uncle William. Tom was an orphan who had lost both parents four years ago. Nancy shivered as she thought how dreadful that would be. Fortunately, Tom's care had been taken over by the vestry of Blisland Parish Church. They aided their deceased members' orphans by helping them to learn a trade. Tom had been apprenticed to Uncle William at the Geddy foundry.

Nancy knew that Tom's apprenticeship meant that legally he must perform faithfully the work Uncle William assigned to him. But, on the other hand, Uncle William had a legal obligation, too. During the years that Tom was in service to him, Uncle William would have to teach him the founder's trade. By the time Tom was grown and had served his years as an apprentice, he would be a skilled and competent journeyman.

Nancy allowed Jamie to walk the short distance

from the house to the foundry, but she carried him in her arms as she entered her uncles' foundry. It was a bustling, busy, noisy place. Hard at work were her father's older brothers, Uncle William and Uncle David; George, their slave, who was skilled as a blacksmith; two journeymen; and two apprentices. At times Nancy's father worked at the forge, but she saw no sign of him now, which meant he was probably working in the shop.

Her cousin William junior, the other apprentice, almost ran past her, then came to a skidding stop. "Good day to you, Nancy!" he cried. "I can't stop to talk! I've been sent on an errand."

Nancy smiled as she watched him dash from the foundry. Errands or not, William was always in a hurry. He was one of the first to arrive at the foundry in the morning and often the last to leave in the evening. He seemed eager to progress beyond the early and boring tasks of lighting fires, polishing the finished castings, pumping the bellows, bringing in coal for the forge, and sweeping the floor.

Tom put down the candlestick he'd been polishing and motioned to Nancy to join him.

Jamie smiled and held out his arms to Tom. Like Nancy, he had a special liking for Tom.

Tom grinned as he took Jamie into his arms. He

gave him a quick hug, then handed him back to Nancy and returned to his polishing.

Nancy took a deep breath and said in a rush, "I don't think that feeling ill is an excuse for speaking sharply to people. Do you?"

Tom looked up. "What did your stepmother say to you?"

"Why, how did you know I was speaking about my stepmother?"

Tom's eyes crinkled as he smiled. "It was not hard to guess. What did she say?"

"She asked me to take care of Jamie," Nancy replied. "It was not the words she said. It was her tone of voice."

"Because she felt ill?"

"Feeling ill is not an excuse," Nancy repeated.

For a moment Tom rubbed diligently at the candle-stick, which had begun to gleam in the flickering light from the forge. Finally he asked, "How did you behave toward others when you were ill?"

Startled, Nancy blurted out, "I've never been ill. That is, not really ill. A winter sniffle at the most."

"Then you would have to make an effort to understand how an ill person would feel. 'Tis hard, is it not?"

Nancy sighed. "To be truthful, I've never tried."

"Perhaps you should."

Jamie began to squirm in Nancy's arms. "Down," he demanded.

Nancy tried to look hurt, but she couldn't. Instead she smiled at Tom. "I came to you because I wanted a little sympathy. Instead you gave me a lecture."

Tom grinned at her. "You didn't need sympathy," he said.

Jamie wiggled so hard that Nancy had to hold him tightly. "The forge is no place for you," she said to him. "Perhaps when I've finished my chores I'll have time to take you for a walk."

"Good luck with your stepmother," Tom called as Nancy turned to go.

With a last smile at Tom, Nancy carried Jamie back to the house.

In spite of her good intentions, it wasn't until late afternoon that Nancy had time to take Jamie outside to enjoy what was left of the cool, sunny day. Nancy took his hand and led him out the front door of their house onto Duke of Gloucester Street.

With a gasp Nancy jumped aside as two angry men ran past. Many others were in the street, and they seemed to be heading in the direction of the

Capitol. From the way they were dressed, Nancy could see that many in the crowd were men of property, so it surprised her that they were shouting. Nancy couldn't tell what they were angry about, and she was curious, so she held Jamie's hand tightly and followed them.

As she passed Wetherburn's Tavern, she heard someone call, "Nancy! Wait!"

Nancy stopped and turned. Running toward her was her friend Harry Armistead, Mrs. Wetherburn's tall, husky twelve-year-old grandson.

After his father had become seriously ill, about five years earlier, Harry had been sent from his parents' Charles City plantation to Williamsburg to live with his grandmother and her husband. His step-grandfather and then his father had died, but Harry had not returned to Charles City to live with his mother. Why would anyone choose to be separated from his mother? Nancy wondered. Perhaps it wasn't Harry's choice. Nancy was much too polite to ask Harry, although she was terribly curious.

As Harry slid to a stop beside her, she said, "I thought you no longer lived with your grandmother. Didn't you only last month begin boarding at the college's grammar school?"

"I did, but—"

"Then why are you here?"

"We have days off, Nancy." Harry made a face at her. "Now, will you stop talking and listen to what I have to say? It's important. You and Jamie must return home."

"Why?" Nancy asked. "What's happening?"

Instead of answering, Harry asked, "Where's your father?"

"Papa? He's working in the shop. Why?"

"And your uncle William and your uncle David?"

"In the foundry." Nancy sighed with exasperation. "Harry! Stop beating about the bush and tell me what is taking place." She caught herself and lowered her voice. "Please to tell me, Harry," she said.

Harry stood as tall as he could for his twelve years, as though he were trying to look as important as his news. "Colonel George Mercer arrived in Williamsburg a short time ago," he said.

Nancy knew all about Colonel Mercer and his tax-collecting duties as the stamp agent for Virginia. In April, when the colonists had heard that Parliament had passed the Stamp Act, most of the adults Nancy knew had complained angrily.

"Parliament has no authority to tax Virginians," Mr. Powell had declared. "Virginians elect no representatives to Parliament. It is our right as

Englishmen to be taxed *only* by our elected representatives. Therefore only the House of Burgesses can tax Virginians."

Mr. Greenhow, the merchant who lived across the street from the Geddys, had spoken in a similar vein. "I am shocked that the king would permit such a law. But even if the Stamp Act has His Majesty's support, we cannot stand by idly while Britain violates our rights.

"The law will affect almost every Virginian," he had complained. "We will be required to put tax stamps on all manner of items—newspapers, pamphlets, legal papers, even the playing cards I sell in my store—and as a result, they will cost more."

"The Stamp Act," Nancy said to Harry. "Is that what this commotion is all about?"

"Yes," Harry answered. "When Colonel Mercer passed the Exchange a short time ago, looking for Lieutenant Governor Fauquier, some of the merchants and gentlemen followed him yelling that the Stamp Act was wrong. Other men have joined in, and you can see how angry everyone is. Colonel Mercer continued on his way and is now with the lieutenant governor on the steps of the coffeehouse next to the Exchange." He glanced down the street. "The crowd seems to be waiting."

Nancy knew that the Exchange was an open area in front of the Capitol wall at the end of Duke of Gloucester Street. There merchants met to set prices on agricultural products and conduct financial exchanges.

Nancy studied Harry. "How do you know all that has happened?" she demanded.

"A visitor at the tavern told us." Harry frowned as he added, "You're only a girl, Nancy. You don't belong in this crowd. If there's trouble, you could be in danger."

"Up, Nancy. Up." Jamie tugged at Nancy's hand, and she bent to lift him. She was glad of the diversion. She didn't want to answer Harry until she'd had time to think.

"Your father should be here, not you," Harry said.

Nancy took a deep breath, angry at Harry for criticizing her father. Her father never discussed such serious matters in Nancy's presence, so she didn't know what his position on the Stamp Act or anything else was.

Suddenly Nancy was aware that the crowd was quieting. "Come, Harry," she said. "Let's move closer. Governor Fauquier has stepped out of the group of men on the porch of the coffeehouse, and he looks as if he's preparing to speak. I want to hear what he'll say."

Tucking Jamie tightly in one arm, she grabbed Harry's hand. As she ducked through the crowd she pulled and tugged Harry along behind her until they were close to the steps of the coffeehouse.

The lieutenant governor, who stood in front of the handful of men on the porch, raised both hands and pleaded with the crowd for silence.

But voices rose from the crowd. "We asked Mercer to tell us—will he enforce the Stamp Act or will he resign?"

"He wouldn't answer us, Governor Fauquier. He said he'd give us his answer Friday. Friday is too late! The act will go into effect on Friday—November first."

"We want an answer now, sir!"

"Yes! Now!"

Lieutenant Governor Fauquier took another step forward, so he was standing slightly in front of Colonel Mercer and the men on the porch who were talking with him. Just then another voice shouted, "See how the governor takes care of him!"

As if propelled by an angry blast of air, the crowd seemed to surge forward, and Nancy lost her grip on Harry. She clutched Jamie tightly as she was pushed forward, too. Perhaps Harry had been right and she should have stayed out of harm's way. Nancy could feel a growing anger in the men who pressed closely around her. She suddenly recalled reports that in August a crowd in Boston had destroyed the homes of men thought to support the Stamp Act and threatened their lives. She gasped as it suddenly occurred to her that Colonel Mercer's life might be in danger.

Surely these men would do nothing so rash. Fearful of what might happen, Nancy tried to elbow her way out of the crowd, but she couldn't. The men had massed together thickly. Like it or not, she was trapped.

Chapter Three

Jamie squirmed in her arms and complained. "Down, down," he repeated.

"Not now, Jamie," Nancy said. She bounced him up and down to comfort him.

Lieutenant Governor Fauquier took another step that carried him to the very edge of the porch. His gaze pierced the crowd as he seemed to search for those he knew to be responsible citizens, meeting them eye to eye.

The crowd responded, and Nancy wasn't surprised. The lieutenant governor was generally liked and respected. The people slowly quieted and allowed him to speak.

"You will not have to wait until Friday for Colonel

Mercer's answer," Lieutenant Governor Fauquier told them. "Because of the entreaties of his friends, Colonel Mercer has promised you an answer at the Capitol tomorrow evening at five o'clock. Before that time he and I will meet to discuss the situation."

Here and there in the crowd Nancy heard a few grumbles and muttered complaints, but she realized that the lieutenant governor had eased their anger. Her rapid heartbeat began to settle down. She felt confident Colonel Mercer's life would be spared.

Lieutenant Governor Fauquier raised his voice again.

"It will soon grow dark. I will walk with Colonel Mercer to my house, which means that we will pass among you. I believe no man here would do me any hurt. I trust you to allow me to conduct Colonel Mercer in safety."

Nancy held her breath as the lieutenant governor and Colonel Mercer walked down the steps of the porch and into the crowd.

As people stepped aside to let them through, Lieutenant Governor Fauquier strode bravely, back straight and head held high. Colonel Mercer quickly followed. He looked straight ahead, his face grim.

For a moment Nancy pitied him. Colonel Mercer

was not the source of the trouble. Others had initiated and passed the hated Stamp Act. Colonel Mercer had only been appointed to carry it out. Nancy realized that at another time such an appointment would have been an honor for Colonel Mercer and his family.

Would the men in the crowd, if the lieutenant governor had not calmed them, have let their anger destroy their senses? Would they have taken Colonel Mercer's life? "No! They couldn't!" Nancy whispered aloud. She shivered.

As the crowd began to thin, Nancy hurried toward her home. She was anxious to discuss with her father what had happened. Harry, who tried to match her rapid steps, couldn't stop talking about what had happened.

"We gave that Colonel Mercer something to think about," he bragged. "He now knows that he cannot advance his own interests at the expense of his fellow Virginians." He chuckled. "Didn't he look exactly like a rabbit cornered by a fox?"

"He did not appear fearful to me," Nancy said. "But I was."

Harry allowed himself a slight smile. "I told you girls didn't belong in that crowd."

"I belonged there as much as you did," Nancy snapped.

With a surprised glance, Harry said, "That's where you're wrong. In only nine years I will reach my majority, complete my education, be able to buy property, and vote. But even before then I can lend my support to the other loyal men of Virginia. You're only a girl, so your support doesn't matter."

Nancy clamped her teeth together in frustration. She knew that many spinsters and widows, including her own grandmother, conducted business. And her father had once told her that after his own father died, Grandmother had petitioned the House of Burgesses to pay her the money owed her late husband. When the burgesses refused, she petitioned again, and the burgesses agreed to pay the debt. But it was true that Grandmother could not vote and that Nancy would never be able to, either. Nancy also knew that when she married, her husband would control any property they owned.

"Women have opinions, too," she snapped at Harry.

He raised one eyebrow. "Well? What is your opinion? Do you wish Colonel Mercer to see that the Stamp Act is carried out?"

Nancy sighed. "I need to learn more," she said. "At this point I truly don't know."

They reached the steps of Wetherburn's Tavern, and Harry said, "Come in for tea. Grandmother has made some plum tarts."

For an instant Nancy's mouth watered. She could almost taste the sweet plum pastries. But she shook her head. "Thank you, but I must take Jamie home," she answered.

She put Jamie on his feet and followed his path, which veered as he examined a spider on a gatepost, jumped into a drift of dried leaves, and chased a boy rolling a hoop.

Nancy kept a close eye on him while she thought about what she had seen and heard. She wondered if her father had been wise to stay at his work. Or, on the other hand, had he been unpatriotic to the Virginia colony by not showing his support?

Nancy didn't go into the house when she returned home. She knew her father would not leave his shop until it was evening and time for supper. But she was desperate to speak with someone about the scene at the Exchange. Instead, she took Jamie back to the foundry, joining Tom at a table from which he was cleaning sand, making it ready for the next morning's work.

"What was all that noise in the streets?" Tom asked Nancy. "Did you see what was taking place?"

"I was there," Nancy answered. She told him about Colonel Mercer's frightening reception.

Tom listened intently, then spoke in a low voice. "I've heard your father talking to his brothers. If the stamp agent is not allowed to do his job of distributing the stamps, the courts will close. Master James is afraid that if the courts close, people will not be able to collect the debts owed to them. They will not have the money to buy his silverwork or the pieces he imports from England. Many people are already concerned because tobacco prices have fallen during the last two years and their crops are earning less money. Now, with all of the uncertainty about the Stamp Act, they may decide that it is frivolous to pay your father to remake their old silver pieces into new styles."

Nancy breathed a quick sigh. So that was it! Worry about his livelihood was what had held her father back from joining in the protest.

Tom's forehead wrinkled in worry. "Those whose businesses fail may be unable to support apprentices."

"Tom!" Nancy cried. "Surely you don't think that—"

Elizabeth suddenly called from the doorway,

"Nancy, why must I always search for you? Where have you been for so long?"

Nancy whirled to face her. "I took Jamie for a walk," she said.

Jamie smiled and held out his arms. "Mama!" he called.

"I need you to help prepare supper," Elizabeth said complainingly to Nancy.

"It was a pleasant afternoon," Nancy said. "I told you I would take Jamie for a walk."

"A *brief* walk. I didn't expect you to be gone so long." Elizabeth sighed. "If you could only understand how ill I feel!"

"Mama!" Jamie repeated. He eagerly bounced up and down in Nancy's arms.

Nancy hurried to Elizabeth and shoved Jamie at her. Admittedly Elizabeth was pale, but was she as ill as she claimed? Nancy thought about Tom's suggestion. Perhaps if she tried to put herself in Elizabeth's place . . .

"And Jamie is filthy. How could you let him get so dirty, Nancy?" Elizabeth began, but Nancy didn't answer. Angrily she strode from the foundry across the yard into the kitchen.

Chapter Four

At supper that night Nancy recounted to her father and Elizabeth all she had seen and heard in the encounter with Colonel Mercer. "You should have been there, Papa," she said.

Mr. Geddy paused, his knife poised over his slice of mutton. "I had much work to do," he answered. He returned to cutting his meat.

"Papa, it seemed that most of the men of Williamsburg joined in the protest," Nancy said. "They demanded to know if the stamp agent would resign, and they were upset because he wouldn't give them an answer."

Elizabeth stared at Nancy in distress. "I can't believe you would take little Jamie into an angry crowd."

Nancy began, "But I was holding him in my arms—"

Elizabeth pressed a hand to her abdomen. "What you have told me is very upsetting, and I have been cautioned not to become unduly upset. We will speak no more of this unfortunate incident," she said. "Do you understand?"

Nancy glanced once more at her father, who steadily concentrated on his mutton, not looking up. "Yes," she sighed. "I understand."

Later, after the supper dishes had been washed and put away, Nancy sat by her father in the dining room. Elizabeth and Jamie were not in the room, and Nancy was delighted. This was the way it had often been before Elizabeth came to stay, with only the two of them together. Now, perhaps, she could get the answers to her questions.

"Papa," Nancy said bluntly, "last week Hannah Powell told me that her father quoted to his family from Patrick Henry's speeches against the Stamp Act in the House of Burgesses. She asked me at the time if you were in sympathy with those who oppose the Stamp Act. I told her I didn't know.

"Our neighbor, Mr. Greenhow, also argues against the Stamp Act. I heard him tell someone that the colonists should not have to pay a tax that they did not agree to. But I have not heard you speak out—even in private to me. Today Harry Armistead also asked me about your position, and I had no answer for him, either."

Mr. Geddy looked at Nancy gravely, then said, "Resisting our king and Parliament can lead to some serious consequences. If we do not follow the terms of the Stamp Act, there is every possibility that Virginia's courts will be closed, ships will not be able to leave the harbor, and merchants will not be able to conduct business. Many innocent people will be harmed."

"I'm puzzled, Papa," Nancy said. "All the men who protested today agreed that the Stamp Act is wrong. So if the Stamp Act is wrong, then it must be opposed. Is that not right?"

"Is it right for Virginians to be harmed in the ways I have explained?"

Nancy thought a moment. "Perhaps for a while, at least, if it leads to Parliament and the king's abolishing the Stamp Act."

Mr. Geddy looked even more solemn. "Have you considered that during that time of waiting some men might have great difficulty keeping their businesses operating? They may even find it impossible to feed and clothe their families. And what if this protest fails to move Parliament and the king and they stand fast on the Stamp Act?"

Nancy drew a deep breath. If people would have trouble taking care of their own family, then certainly apprentices would be in a great deal of trouble. "I'm worried about Tom, Papa. If Uncle William's business fails, he might no longer be able to keep Tom as an apprentice. I must talk to Uncle William and ask him if—"

"No!" Mr. Geddy interrupted. "Only in the most dire situation would your uncle fail to meet his obligations to Tom. In such an event, your concern should be for your uncle William and his family— your own relations. They would be suffering greatly. The Blisland church vestry might be able to apprentice Tom to another tradesman, but your uncle William could expect little assistance. Do I have your promise that you will not speak to your uncle William about Tom?"

"Yes, Papa," Nancy answered quietly. She leaned to rest her head on her father's shoulder. "There are so many questions, and I don't know the answers."

"Neither do I," Mr. Geddy murmured. "I can only try to do my best. Life should be peaceful, child, without the turmoil or agitation Mr. Patrick Henry seems to desire. 'Tis true we have no representatives in Parliament who have agreed to the Stamp Act. Yet I am certain that Parliament, the king, and his ministers have our best interests at heart."

Pride in her father swelled up like a bubble, warming Nancy's heart. "I love you, Papa," she said.

"I love you, too, daughter," he answered.

For a long time Nancy snuggled against her father, as content as she had been before Elizabeth's arrival. No matter what the protest of the Stamp Act would bring, Nancy was sure that Papa would do what was right.

The next morning everyone at the market had an opinion to offer about what Colonel Mercer would do.

Nancy walked home slowly, carrying her purchases. Questions raced through her mind. Without a stamp agent, what would happen to her father's business? Would customers no longer be able to afford to have their gold and silver redesigned? Would Nancy's father be unable to receive beautiful objects from England to sell in his shop because there were no stamp agents?

As she reached the corner across from her home, she saw Mr. Greenhow standing on the front steps of his store. Talking with a handful of customers gathered below the steps, he stated his conviction that Colonel Mercer would resign.

Passing through the small crowd of shoppers, Nancy recognized Mrs. Anne Nicholas and her good friend Mrs. Martha Gooseley, who lived in Yorktown but often visited Williamsburg. Even though Mrs. Gooseley had a strident, carrying voice, Nancy tried not to listen to her comments.

Nancy was about to cross the street when Mrs. Gooseley's words startled her. "I understand that the Geddy brothers refused to join the protest," she said.

"Now, madam," Mrs. Nicholas began, but her friend spoke even more insistently.

"Which means, my dear, that many citizens in Williamsburg will think twice about bringing their business to the Geddys."

Nancy froze. She could feel her heart beat rapidly, and for a moment it was hard to breathe.

Mrs. Nicholas calmly answered, "Some of the Geddys' customers may have problems because their debt claims can't be processed in the courts, which were closed when the Stamp Act was passed. But I haven't heard that—"

Mrs. Gooseley sniffed. "Well, *I* have. There's talk that there may be major trouble for the foundry."

"Oh!" Nancy sucked in her breath.

Mrs. Nicholas looked in Nancy's direction, then quickly turned to put a hand on her friend's arm. Nancy heard her say, "Be quiet, Martha, I pray you. The child can hear you."

Nancy hurried across the street toward home. Was Mrs. Gooseley right? Would the Geddys' businesses suffer? And despite her father's assurances, Nancy remained concerned about Tom's welfare, too.

As soon as Nancy had eaten breakfast and helped Grace straighten the dining room, she hurried out to the forge. Her father was not there, but Tom was hard at work. He swept with such vigor that he didn't look up even when Nancy called his name.

"Mr. Greenhow believes the stamp agent will resign and leave Williamsburg," Nancy told him.

Tom stopped sweeping, brushed a strand of hair from his eyes, and said, "We heard the rumors."

"What will it mean? What will you do? Mrs. Gooseley thinks the foundry will lose business because Papa and Uncle William are not protesting the Stamp Act."

Tom's eyes darkened. "'Tis true there were very few customers yesterday and none yet this morning," he said, "but that could be only coincidence."

"Is that what you really think?" Nancy asked.

Tom slowly shook his head. "Business is off. For what reason I do not know."

"Tom, we can't let this happen. Perhaps I can convince Papa to take a stand against the Stamp Act. This may influence my uncles to do the same."

"How can you do this?" Tom asked.

Nancy shrugged. "I do not know." She raised her head to look at Tom. "You always have so many good ideas—surely *you* must have an idea of how this could be done."

Tom frowned as he thought, and Nancy held her breath, waiting for his answer. Finally he said, "Master William told us not to dwell on what could happen tomorrow, Nancy. We have much work that must be done today, and that is all we should think about. We will hope for the best."

Tom looked so unhappy, Nancy wished she had not been the bearer of such troubling news.

Nancy walked toward the house, trying to apply Tom's advice. She, too, would try not to dwell on what might happen. She'd think only about the work that must be done today.

It was still early, not yet time to go to Mrs. Powell's house for her cooking lesson. If she worked quickly, she'd complete her chores, and Elizabeth would find no reason to object to the lesson. Just outside the kitchen, she came face to face with Elizabeth, Jamie in tow.

Jamie tugged at Elizabeth's hand, complaining loudly. "Ball," he insisted. "Play ball."

Elizabeth's face was twisted with exhaustion and impatience. "Stop fussing, Jamie!" she exclaimed.

Couldn't Elizabeth see that Jamie just wanted to be played with? Nancy scooped up Jamie and swung him from side to side until he forgot he'd been unhappy and squealed with laughter.

"Which would you like me to do?" Nancy asked Elizabeth. "Keep Jamie busy or prepare the beef and vegetables for dinner?"

Elizabeth sighed and rested a hand on Nancy's arm. In a low, confiding voice she said, "I have always hoped I'd be strong enough to endure anything, but I did not know that bearing children would be so difficult. Most women can manage. I don't know why it should be different with me."

"I'm sorry," Nancy said, surprised when Elizabeth's gaze softened. She was no longer the stern, unsmiling stepmother. She was like a hurt child needing sympathy.

"Why don't you put on your cloak and go for a

brisk walk?" Nancy suggested. "The air is cool and clear and will do you good. I'll put the beef on to boil and prepare the potatoes and carrots. Grace will help me keep an eye on Jamie."

Elizabeth hesitated. "He probably needs a dry clout."

"I can change it."

"The bedding needs airing. And the linens must be folded—"

"I have done all these chores before," Nancy interrupted. "I did them—and did them well—before you . . ." Her voice trailed off. *Before you came to live with us?* No. Nancy couldn't finish the sentence. She wished she had never begun it, as Elizabeth's gaze grew defensive.

Elizabeth took a deep breath and reached for Jamie, tugging the protesting child from Nancy's arms. "I'll go for a walk, and I'll take Jamie with me. Please assist Grace in the kitchen."

Nancy sighed. Hadn't she just offered to help Elizabeth? She had truly wanted to help her. Why, oh why, had she been given a stepmother who was determined to be difficult? Why couldn't her own beautiful mother have lived? Why couldn't her loving grandmother have stayed with her son and granddaughter and not moved away?

Why, why, why? There were no answers. Glumly

Nancy entered the kitchen, ready to help prepare the food for dinner.

Later, as Nancy walked from the kitchen to the house, Elizabeth returned with a sleepy Jamie and murmured, "I'll put him down to nap. Let us air the bedding tomorrow."

Nancy took a quick, excited breath. "Then may I visit the Powells? Mrs. Powell has promised to teach me to make mince pie."

Elizabeth's face showed her surprise as she stopped and faced Nancy. "I've told you *I* would like to teach you to bake. I'm as fine a teacher as Annabelle Powell. If you would but listen to me, I could teach you to bake a queen's cake, with the same receipt my mother used to teach me."

For a moment Nancy didn't answer. If Elizabeth were to insist on teaching her, she'd listen, and she'd follow instructions well, but learning from Elizabeth wouldn't be fun. With Hannah, Ann, and Mrs. Powell, baking would be like a party. "I thank you," Nancy said politely. "Perhaps when you aren't so tired we could have a lesson. For now, though, may I please visit the Powells?"

Elizabeth sighed, and under Jamie's weight, her shoulders drooped. "You may go," she said. She turned and walked toward the house.

"I thank you," Nancy repeated as Elizabeth walked away. She took two steps after Elizabeth, knowing she had displeased her stepmother, probably even hurt her feelings. Nancy wanted to make everything right between them again, but she couldn't think of what to say. She turned and hurried as fast as she could toward the Powells' home on Waller Street.

When Nancy arrived, Annabelle Powell, Hannah, and Ann greeted her warmly and led her through the house to the kitchen outbuilding. The room was large and cheerful, with a huge fireplace and plenty of space to work.

Mrs. Powell had already placed the butter, the flour, and a pitcher of water on one of the tables. She instructed the girls to sift a quart of flour through a sieve, then gently divide it between four large bowls.

"I don't think the measurements will be right," Hannah said with a giggle. "Some of the flour has ended up on Ann's apron and Nancy's nose."

"And your own forehead," Nancy said with a grin. "Wait till you spy yourself in a looking glass."

"My nose itches," Ann complained.

"Don't rub it now, with all that flour on your hands," Hannah said.

"But I—I must sneeze!"

"No!" they all shouted. Just in time Mrs. Powell

grabbed Ann's shoulders and turned her away from the cones of powdery flour.

Nancy laughed so hard she doubled over. Aiming for a stool to sit on, she missed and landed on the floor.

Hannah joined her, laughing until tears came to her eyes.

As she wiped Hannah's eyes with a corner of her apron, Mrs. Powell tried to sound stern. "Come, come, girls. Tend to business. We must put our mince pies together and into the oven."

Soon they were adding butter to the flour, stirring in small amounts of water, and working it all together with their hands.

Somehow they managed to roll the sticky dough into circles on the floured table, placing half of the circles in pie pans. The mince filling was carefully spooned into the shells, then strips of dough laid on top to form a lattice design. Nancy carefully pinched together the bottom crust and top strips where they met on the edges of her pie.

As Mrs. Powell placed the pies in the brick oven, Nancy, Hannah, and Ann grinned at each other.

"You are wearing as much dough as went into the piecrusts," Nancy said to Ann. She tried to remove a smear of sticky dough from Ann's cheek but only seemed to add to it, making it larger.

Hannah twirled around the room. "We have decorated ourselves for the twelve days of Christmas," she said, and began to sing "The Holly and the Ivy."

"If it's music you want, then suppose you wash your hands and faces and remove your soiled aprons," Mrs. Powell told them. "We'll leave the servant to clean the kitchen and take the pies from the oven when they are done. While we're waiting, we can gather around the spinet harpsichord and practice singing the Christmas songs from Isaac Watts's book of hymns."

Soon, scrubbed and joyful, Nancy wrapped her arms around Hannah's and Ann's shoulders, singing "While Shepherds Watched Their Flocks." The late-morning sun lit the airy parlor with gold, and the light notes of the harpsichord danced into the air. What could be more perfect?

Nancy was ready to leave when Mrs. Powell handed her the pie she had made. It was well wrapped and warm in her hands. "I'm eager to share the pie with my father," Nancy said.

"And your mother," Mrs. Powell added with a smile. "How is she faring?"

With a sharp pang of guilt Nancy realized she hadn't given Elizabeth a single thought during the entire morning. "She does not feel well," Nancy admitted. "When she was expecting Jamie she felt ill the entire time. I suppose this illness will be the same as when she was carrying Jamie."

"The poor dear," Mrs. Powell said. She patted Nancy's shoulder. "She is certainly lucky to have you to help her. I know you are taking especially good care of her."

"I do what I can," Nancy murmured.

After she had thanked Mrs. Powell again and said good-bye to Hannah and Ann, Nancy walked home quickly. *Well, it's true,* she argued with herself. *I do my chores. I help wherever I can. If I can't please Elizabeth, it's not my fault.*

The morning was over, and with it the joy and laughter. It hadn't been like this before Papa married Elizabeth, Nancy thought. Wasn't the situation at home ever going to get better?

Chapter Five

After dinner, as Nancy cut her pie into wedges and served them, she was so excited that her hands trembled.

Her father slowly ate the first bite, savoring the taste. "Excellent! Excellent!" he exclaimed after he had swallowed. "The crust is light and firm. No one could have made it better."

Nancy beamed and turned to Elizabeth for further praise.

But Elizabeth frowned and removed a tiny clove from her mouth.

"I'm afraid you did not carefully grind the spices," she told Nancy. "A good cook always performs even the slightest details with diligence. This is something you must learn."

Elizabeth's criticism stung. "I didn't make the mince filling," Nancy said. "Mrs. Powell did. Hannah, Ann, and I only made the pie dough."

Elizabeth nodded. For just an instant Nancy thought she saw a look of satisfaction on her face. "Then you did well," Elizabeth said. "The crust has a good texture for a first try. As you continue to practice, you'll improve."

At least she had a compliment for the crust, Nancy thought, surprising herself with her desire to win Elizabeth's good opinion. Apparently what Elizabeth thought mattered more to Nancy than she had realized.

She saw her father watching her with a pleading look in his eyes. "I thank you," Nancy managed to say, keeping her voice calm. "I'll remember your advice when I bake during Christmastide."

Elizabeth pushed her plate of half-eaten pie to one side. "There will be no need for special baking and cooking," she said, looking away from Nancy. "I'm afraid I'm not up to entertaining company during this coming Christmas season."

Nancy's mouth dropped open in surprise. When she was able to speak she protested, "But during the twelve days of Christmas we are bound to have visitors. Perhaps we could invite friends to a simple dinner. Mrs. Powell will teach me to prepare the fancier dishes, so I can supervise Grace as she cooks the food."

Elizabeth mutely shook her head.

Nancy took a deep breath to steady herself. "'Tis not yet Advent, not until December first. By Christmas day you will probably be in much better health."

Nancy heard the rising hope in her own voice, but Elizabeth did not seem to share her optimism. "'Twill be better not to count on Christmas festivities," Elizabeth said quietly.

"Papa?" Nancy pleaded. "Are we to have no Christmas festivities at all?"

"We will abide by your mother's wishes," he answered. He placed his napkin by his plate and added, "Since we have finished, let us say our prayer of thanksgiving and be excused." Without a pause, he bowed his head and quickly began the prayer.

Nancy barely heard her father's words or noticed when he was finished. As her father and Elizabeth left the room, she sank back in her chair. Her slice of untasted mince pie, which had once seemed so glorious, now looked cold and lumpy, forlorn in the middle of its plate.

The Christmas season should be a time of great happiness, Nancy thought. Festivities would begin on Christmas day. Relatives would arrive from out of town. Friends would dine at each other's homes. People would be invited to tea and to sing Christmas carols. And gifts—usually coins—would be given by parents or masters to their children, slaves, servants, and apprentices. Papa would give gifts of coins to Nancy, Jamie, and Grace. There would be sweet-meats, many good things to eat, visitors to share the joy. . . .

But not this Christmas. And all because of Elizabeth.

Nancy picked up her slice of pie, chose a clean fork and napkin, and carried them out to the forge to give to Tom.

Although it was part of Uncle William's duty to feed Tom, Nancy liked to bring him special treats. On every day except Sunday, when the forge was closed, he worked twelve to fourteen hours. All that work, plus the fact that he was a growing boy, meant that he was always hungry.

Tom's eyes brightened when he saw the mince pie, but he said, "I do not recall your bringing me mince pie before. Why are we having it now?"

"I'm learning baking skills," Nancy said. "Next week Mrs. Powell will teach me to make custards."

Tom devoured the pie, smacking his lips. "This pie is the best I ever ate," he said. "Well, maybe second-best. It's almost as good as the mince pies my mother made." He threw a quick glance at Nancy as he added, "Though I do believe your crust is lighter."

"Elizabeth actually did praise the crust—for a beginning effort," Nancy complained with a wry smile. "But she found fault with the filling. The spices were not ground to her satisfaction."

Tom licked the fork. "They were to mine," he said happily. Then he became serious. "Nancy, the concerns you have with Mistress Geddy . . . Why don't you dwell only on her words of praise and forget the rest? Perhaps she did not mean to criticize and meant only to teach."

"Oh, Tom," Nancy replied. "I truly want to think only good of Elizabeth, but when she scolds or admonishes—"

"Sometimes," Tom interrupted, "that is what a mother must do to instruct a child in what should or should not be done." He chuckled. "I remember how my worried mother admonished my brother and me when we climbed on the roof of our house in order to see into a bird's nest we had glimpsed tucked into a niche in the chimney."

Nancy smiled. "You are fortunate to have memories of your mother," she said. "When my mother died, I wasn't old enough to remember her."

"Memories make the leaving harder," Tom said softly.

"But having nothing to hold on to is worse," Nancy told him. "Your mother can live on through you and your memories."

"You don't even remember your mother holding you and reading to you?"

Shaking her head, Nancy answered, "No. I only remember my grandmother doing those things."

"I'm sorry," Tom said.

Touched by his sympathy, Nancy reached out, resting a hand on Tom's arm. "Tom," she said, "had you no relatives who could have taken you in?"

"Not in the colonies," Tom said. "There were an old aunt and a few cousins in England, but they could not afford to pay the passage back for me and my brother, or keep us once we'd arrived."

He licked a finger and used it to pick up the last small crumb on the plate. Eating the crumb from his finger, he said, "The Blisland Parish vestry was able to place my brother near our old home in New Kent

County, but they were obliged to send me here, many hours away. I used to cry at night, because I felt so lonely and afraid, but I don't cry any longer. The people at the church found a good place for me. I feel as though you are my family now. Master William is a fair and good master. And I am learning a trade I know I will like. Someday I will be a master craftsman and perhaps have my own forge and shop.

"But there are times," he admitted, "when I miss my mother and father so much that it hurts terribly."

Nancy fought back the tears that burned behind her eyes. Silently she promised herself that she would do all in her power to protect Tom from what might happen to his apprenticeship because of the Stamp Act.

"Tom," one of the journeymen called from the forge, "I need you on the bellows."

Without another word to Nancy, Tom ran to grasp the handles on the bellows and began to pump them up and down.

Nancy took the plate and fork to the kitchen, where Grace had almost finished washing the plates.

Grace glanced at the plate, then gave Nancy a conspiratorial smile. "Did Master Tom like the pie?" she asked.

Nancy smiled back. "Oh, yes. Whatever I have

brought him, Tom has liked. He loves to eat—especially sweets."

"Your pie was good," Grace said. "I stole a taste."

"Eat as much of it as you like," Nancy said. She sighed in discouragement. "It will not be served in this house again."

Nancy didn't want to think about Elizabeth's opinion of her pie. Tom was enough to worry about. "It is sad that Tom has lost both of his parents," she said.

As Grace silently placed the clean kitchenware in the cupboard, Nancy thought for the first time about Grace's family. She had parents, yet Nancy had never asked about them. Nancy had never even wondered about them.

"Grace," she asked bluntly, "are your mother and father living?"

"I hope so, Mistress Nancy," Grace said quietly.

"Don't you know?"

Grace shook her head. "When the man who owned my family died, my father was sold to someone who lives somewhere in one of the western counties of Virginia. My mother went to an old couple—the Josiah Barkers—who live in Richmond. Your father bought me."

61

"That was three years ago," Nancy said. "Haven't you heard from your parents since then?"

"How could I hear? I've asked many slaves who have come to town with their owners, but none of them has known either my mother or my father."

"But . . . could you contact someone by post?"

"Mistress Nancy," Grace said, "none of us can read or write."

Shocked, Nancy backed up and sat on a tall stool. With her parents so far away, Grace might just as well be an orphan, like Tom. It didn't matter that Grace was a slave. She had lost her mother and father and must feel the same heartache as Tom. *And I, too,* Nancy thought. *Even though I do not remember my mother, I miss her terribly.*

"Oh, Grace," Nancy said. "What can we do?"

There were tears in Grace's eyes, but she said, "I keep remindin' myself what my mama told me. When I complained about anythin', she always said, 'Child, you must make do.' "

Impatiently Nancy jumped up, shaking her head. "That's not enough, Grace. You don't have to make do. I have just had an idea, and I think it's a good one. Mrs. Anne Wager teaches very young slaves and free blacks to read and write. She would never take a student as old as you, but even if she did, I'm certain Mistress Geddy would not be able to spare you. However, *I* am going to teach you to read and write. Then you can write letters to your parents."

Grace stared in amazement. "But they can't read."

"Surely they'll be able to find someone to read the letters to them."

Grace took a deep breath and clasped her hands together tightly. "Do you mean it, Mistress Nancy? Will you really teach me to read and write?"

"Of course I will," Nancy said. "We'll find time in the kitchen after supper. No one will mind. Are you agreed?"

"Yes, Mistress Nancy," Grace whispered.

Nancy beamed. "Fine. We will begin tomorrow," she said.

As she left the kitchen she continued to smile. She would help Grace learn to read.

In the privacy of her bedchamber Nancy pulled three items from the bottom of her chest of drawers. They were the little hornbook, the slate, and the slate pencil her grandmother had used to teach her to read and write. She could well remember the lessons, even though when they began she was only five. She would follow her grandmother's example and begin by teaching Grace the letters of the alphabet.

Tomorrow, she thought, excited at the idea that she soon would be a teacher. Tomorrow she would begin the lessons that would bring Grace and her mother together again.

Chapter Six

At breakfast Saturday morning Nancy was excited to learn from her father that Colonel Mercer had resigned late Friday afternoon and had left Williamsburg. Perhaps everything would be all right now and Tom could be kept on in his apprenticeship.

"What has happened since Colonel Mercer left Williamsburg?" Nancy began. She served her father the bread Grace had just sliced and made sure a bowl of strawberry jam was within his reach.

"Nothing but talk," Mr. Geddy said. He spread a small piece of bread with sweet butter and jam and chewed it slowly.

"But what will happen? What will we do?" Nancy persisted.

"Until the situation is resolved," her father told her, "we can only continue to produce the items for which we have contracted." Sighing, he put down his knife. Nancy could see the deep concern in his eyes. "Of course, if people cannot collect money owed them or export their crops to England, they will not be able to pay me. I have responsibilities I must meet . . . mouths to feed . . ."

Elizabeth's face was pale as she turned to Nancy. "Please don't worry your father with foolish questions for which there are no answers. We will do as others are doing. We will manage as best we can."

Nancy paid little heed to what Elizabeth had said. Her mind was on what her father had told her, and her main concern was for Tom. "Papa," Nancy asked, "will Uncle William and Uncle David have the same problem at the foundry? And if they do, what will happen to Tom?"

Elizabeth leaned forward, and Nancy could see tears welling in her eyes. "Nancy, I requested you to ask no more questions on this subject. I pray again that you will heed my request."

"But I only—"

Elizabeth sighed unhappily. "You have worried your father. See, he has lost his appetite. Please have the goodness to be silent."

As James Geddy left the table Nancy sat back in her chair, fighting tears. She wasn't hungry, either. She was frightened for Tom—for everyone. All she had wanted was for her father to explain what was taking place. Or perhaps, she admitted to herself, she really wanted him to reassure her that everything would be all right. Did Elizabeth think that because Nancy was still a child she was unaware of political problems?

During the morning, after chores, Nancy worked on the shirt she was making for Jamie. Elizabeth, who was supervising, commented impatiently, "Those stitches are too long. The seam will pull open. You must rip them out and stitch the seam again."

"I've made them as tiny and neat as I could."

"They are not small enough. Try harder."

As Nancy pulled angrily at the thread, she gave a loud sigh of frustration.

Elizabeth looked up from her own sewing. "I was just as resentful as you when my mother ordered me to rip out stitches and do them over—the *correct* way. Someday you will thank me for insisting on perfection, just as I one day thanked my own mother."

Nancy clenched her teeth and rethreaded her needle. *You are not my own mother,* she thought. *And I will never, ever thank you for making me rip out perfectly good stitches.*

Finally Elizabeth folded her own sewing and tucked it into her sewing basket. "I have a headache," she told Nancy. "I'll rest awhile in my bedchamber. Will you please keep a careful eye on Jamie?"

"Gladly," Nancy answered, thankful that the miserable sewing lesson had ended. She stuffed her own sewing into her basket, tucking it on a shelf where Jamie's little hands couldn't get into it.

Nancy's relief soon evaporated as Jamie repeatedly tried to open the drawers of the desk to play with the forbidden items inside them. He cried when Nancy stopped him, he fussed and squirmed when she tried to hold him, and he showed no interest in the toys she offered him.

Just in time Nancy rescued from Jamie's baby hands the book that her father had given her the previous Christmas. As she tucked the book—*Aesop's Fables*—under her skirt and congratulated herself on avoiding a lecture from Elizabeth about taking care of her things, she had an idea.

"I will tell you a story about a greedy fox and a crane with a long bill," she said. She sat Jamie on her lap to face her.

As she went through the tale she used a deep, whining voice for the fox and a high-pitched voice for the crane, making Jamie laugh. Each time the fox tried in vain to drink from the tall-necked jar, Nancy burrowed into Jamie's neck.

Jamie giggled and squealed as Nancy snuggled and played with him. "More," he cried. "More!"

It wasn't until Jamie had thrown his arms around Nancy's neck that she looked up to see Elizabeth watching from the doorway.

"Were we disturbing you?" Nancy asked as she patted Jamie, hushing him.

"No. Of course not," Elizabeth answered. She quickly walked through the passage on the way outside to the kitchen.

For a few moments Nancy held Jamie without moving. She had caught the look of yearning—even a flash of jealousy—that had crossed Elizabeth's face as she stood there watching them play together. For a moment Nancy felt an ache of pity for Elizabeth. Didn't she know how to laugh and tease and have fun? Or was it simply that she didn't want to?

It doesn't matter to me, Nancy told herself, and she pushed away the thought that followed: *Yes, it does.*

Grace's first reading lesson did not go well. Grace was quickly discouraged by how much she would have to learn before she could read. She sighed and put down the hornbook on which the letters of the alphabet were printed. "I can't tell one of these marks from another," she said. "I'll never be able to."

"Yes, you will, because I'll teach you to do so," Nancy said. She leaned closer in the light from the candles she had grouped on the kitchen table. "The first letter is *A*. See . . . you can trace the lines with your finger."

Nancy handed Grace a slate pencil and showed her how to hold it. Then she took Grace's hand in hers and went through the strokes of the *A* on the slate.

"You did it. You wrote an *A*," Nancy said proudly. "Now write over it. Try it alone."

Grace did, again and again. Nancy wiped the slate clean and said, "Now, Grace, remember what you did and write an *A*."

Biting her lip, Grace slowly and neatly wrote the letter *A*.

"You did it!" Nancy cried.

"I did it!" Grace echoed excitedly. She paused a moment, then asked, "Now, what do I do with it?"

"With what?"

"The *A*."

Nancy thought a moment. "You know it so that you recognize it when you are reading or writing."

Grace still seemed puzzled, so Nancy reached for Grace's slate. She printed "I GO TO A MARKET-PLACE," then read it aloud to Grace. "There are your *A*'s," she said.

"Is that one *A* a word?"

"Yes, it's a word."

Grace's eyes widened, and she gave a little jump in her chair. "You mean I wrote a word? I read and wrote a real word?"

"Why, yes, you did," Nancy said.

Grace's voice wobbled. "Oh, Mistress Nancy, I read a whole word! And I wrote it!" She rubbed at her eyes. "I'll learn to read, and I'll write to my mother."

Nancy cleaned the slate again and gave it and the pencil back to Grace. "Let's move on to *B*," she said.

"What word is *B*?" Grace asked.

"*B* isn't a word. It's a letter of the alphabet."

"But *A*'s a word, so why isn't *B* a word?"

Nancy stifled a groan. "Because it just isn't."

"I think it is," Grace said. "I've heard people say it. 'He *be* here tomorrow.' 'He *be* travelin' to Richmond.' "

"No, that's not just the letter *B*. In that word the *B* has an *E* with it."

"Why? It sounds good and clear. It don't need anythin' with it."

"I don't know why. 'Tis just the way it is," Nancy said.

Grace studied the *B*, then shook her head. "Readin' is hard work," she said.

Nancy sighed. "So is teaching," she answered.

Chapter Seven

By Sunday morning, the third of November, people still were asking, "What will happen now that the stamp agent has left Williamsburg?" No one had an answer.

During the week Papa's shop had remained busy. And the foundry, with its clang of hammers, roar of fire, pounding, clinking, whooshing, and thumping, had offered the sounds of normal workdays. But Nancy was aware that not as many customers as usual came to either the forge or her father's shop.

In this case Tom was not a comfort. His own fears added to Nancy's as he quietly told her, "Mrs. Shackleford canceled her order for candlesticks and serving spoons, as did Mr. Abbott for a set of brass harness ornaments."

"They canceled?" Nancy whispered. "Do you think this is the first part of trouble for the foundry that Mrs. Gooseley spoke of?"

Tom shook his head. "I do not know," he said. "There is no way of knowing unless others follow their example."

Nancy clutched Tom's arm. She could feel fear like a cold chill spreading throughout her chest. "We will find a way to change the minds of my father and uncles. They must join the large group of men who have proclaimed their defiance of the Stamp Act. Then they will be accepted and their customers will return."

"How can we do this?" Tom asked. "I have been unable to think of an idea."

Nancy tried to come up with a solution, but she was so frightened that her mind was a muddle, and it was hard to make sense of anything.

"I don't know yet," she told Tom, "but I'll think about what to do. I pray that a good idea will come to me."

But by Sunday—a day of rest, during which the shop and foundry were closed and silent—Nancy still had not come up with the idea she needed.

Nancy dressed in her best gown and hat and, since the day was cool, put on her cloak and mitts. She walked with her family across Palace Street to attend services at Bruton Parish Church.

The Geddys arrived early. Papa liked to greet friends as they arrived in the churchyard. Elizabeth stood by his side, saying little.

Nancy smiled at Tom as he arrived with Uncle William's family, and she greeted Harry, who came with his grandmother.

Brightening as the Powells and Greenhows arrived together, Nancy hurried to join her best friend, Hannah. She couldn't help noticing the warmth and friendliness Mrs. Powell showered on everyone, especially four-year-old Robert and three-year-old Anne Greenhow. Their mother, Judith Greenhow, had died earlier in the year, and since then Mrs. Powell had always paid special attention to them.

Nancy remembered how sad Mrs. Greenhow's death had made Uncle John. She had heard him explain to Elizabeth, "Judith Greenhow was the older sister of Peachy Davenport, one of my best friends when I was growing up. Even though Judith was very proper and Peachy and Ann McKenzie and I were always in one pickle or another, Judith still treated me kindly."

Now, watching Mrs. Powell with Robert and Anne, Nancy knew that her own mother would have been just as caring and friendly to everyone. Why did Elizabeth have to hang back? Why couldn't she smile and chat with everyone? Nancy turned her back on Elizabeth to talk to Hannah. Elizabeth's attitude was too embarrassing. However, Nancy couldn't help overhearing snatches of the group's conversation.

Her father's friends talked about the Stamp Act, which officially had gone into effect on Friday, November 1. There was also much discussion about the Stamp Act Congress, which had convened in New York during most of the month of October. Just two weeks earlier, on October 19, the Congress had adopted a Declaration of Rights and Grievances.

"I strongly protest Governor Fauquier's refusal to call the General Assembly to elect delegates to this congress," Mr. Powell said. "We should have taken part."

"Indeed, sir, we should have," Mr. Greenhow agreed.

"In order to succeed in expressing our views and gaining what we request of the Crown, we must all stand together," someone said.

Someone else spoke in a quiet aside close enough

for Nancy to hear: "The Geddys remain silent. If they are not with us, are they against us?"

With a start Nancy twisted, trying to see who had spoken. But Hannah drew Nancy aside, past one of the high table tombs that stood in the churchyard. "Papa is angry," she said. "He doesn't stop complaining about the unfairness of the Stamp Act and what it might do to harm his business."

Nancy was puzzled. "How could it harm his work of building houses?"

"He might not be able to get the materials or tools he needs from Great Britain," Hannah answered. "And what if people can't collect debts and will have no money to pay for the work he has already done?"

"Oh, I see," Nancy said. "My papa is worried, too, for most of the same reasons. Whoever asked if the Geddys were against the others did not understand."

Hannah put an arm around Nancy's shoulders. "Let's not say another word about the Stamp Act. That is all I hear at home. I can't bear any more of it." She grinned. "Even though Advent will not begin until December first, my mind is already on the Christmas season. Let's talk about what we'll buy with the coins our fathers will give us at Christmastide."

Before Nancy could answer, the church bell began to peal. At the same time a hand gripped her shoulder, and she jumped.

"Come, Nancy," Elizabeth ordered. "Services are ready to begin."

Nancy said a quick good-bye to Hannah and took her place with her family in their pew.

As Lieutenant Governor Fauquier entered to be seated on his special canopied chair, the music of the organ began with a silver note. The music grew, then swirled to fill the church with powerful chords. Nancy closed her eyes, enjoying the skill of the Bruton Parish organist, Peter Pelham.

The services began when the rector, the Reverend James Horrocks, entered the chancel, and Nancy tried to concentrate on the sermon and prayers. However, with Elizabeth solidly beside her, Nancy didn't feel very spiritual.

After church services the Geddy family rode to the home of Nancy's grandmother, Anne Geddy. Nancy was so eager to see her grandmother, she pushed all other thoughts out of her head during the two-hour trip.

As she always did, Grandmother Anne hurried to the front porch and met her son and his family with open arms. While the special hug she had for Nancy nearly took her breath away, the hug Grandmother gave Elizabeth was gentle and tender.

Grandmother peered into Elizabeth's face and tucked in a thin lock of hair that had escaped her cap. "Are you well, Elizabeth?" she asked.

Elizabeth shook her head. "No better than before, thank you."

"Then let's find a comfortable chair for you. Jane will bring you tea with a bit of spearmint in it. Would you also like sugar?" In one swift motion Grandmother reached for Jamie and helped Elizabeth off with her cloak and hat. "Nancy, will you please take care of these?" she asked.

"Sugar?" Jamie repeated to Grandmother. "Sugar?"

Grandmother laughed. "Oh, there'll be sweets for you soon enough, young man. But not until after dinner." Grandmother put an arm around Elizabeth's shoulders and led her into the parlor.

Nancy folded Elizabeth's cloak and put it, with her hat, on a chest. She added her own cloak and hat and walked to the kitchen outbuilding. She didn't want to share her grandmother with Elizabeth, and she knew Grandmother would appear in the kitchen sooner or later.

She found her grandmother already there,

dispatching her slave Jane with Elizabeth's cup of steaming tea.

Nancy snuggled against her grandmother, wrapping her arms around her waist. "I miss you," she said. "I wish you didn't live so far away."

"I miss you, too," Grandmother said. She stepped back, her hands on Nancy's shoulders, her eyes twinkling with excitement. "I'm going to ask your parents if I might have your company for at least four days during the twelve days of Christmas. Would you like to stay with me?"

Nancy bounced on her toes. "Oh, Grandmother! I would love to be with you!"

"Good, because I'm planning to host a ball on Friday, December twenty-seventh—two days after Christmas. I should like you to attend."

Nancy gasped. "A real ball? With musicians?" Her hands flew to her face. "But I have not taken dancing lessons!"

"I think I can teach you all you'd need to know for now. It's not as though you'll be dancing the minuet long into the night. There'll be some country dancing, too, and music and singing of Christmas carols and hymns."

Nancy grabbed her grandmother, hugging her

tightly. "Thank you, Grandmother! I would love to come to your ball!"

Then, just as suddenly, Nancy staggered back a step, her arms dropping to her side. "But I can't. I don't have the proper gown to wear to a ball."

Grandmother smiled. "It so happens I have saved a dress that belonged to your mother. It can be re-made to fit you. It's fashioned of silk brocade the color of cream. Do you think you might like it?"

With a squeal of delight Nancy threw herself at her grandmother again. Off balance, they staggered into a bench and flopped down on it.

"I hope I survive until the ball," Grandmother teased.

"Could we ask Papa now?" Nancy begged. "This very minute?"

Grandmother rose and took Nancy's hand. "Yes, and Elizabeth, too," she said. "They'll also be invited."

For a moment Nancy's stomach grew tight and cold. What if Elizabeth wouldn't allow her to come? If Elizabeth remained at home, would she insist that Nancy stay with her?

Home. Nancy sighed. There would be no Christmas festivities, no guests attending dinners or teas at home.

Quietly Nancy walked to the parlor beside her grandmother, holding her breath as Grandmother Anne repeated her invitation, including Nancy's four-day visit after the ball. She even mentioned the new gown.

James Geddy smiled. "It's hard to believe that Nancy is old enough to attend a ball, but if you think so, madam, then I am in full agreement."

Elizabeth, her eyes on her husband, murmured, "We must decline. My condition will not permit my attending a ball."

"I am sorry you won't feel well enough, Elizabeth," Grandmother said. "However, it's important to me to have Nancy here. If James cannot leave to drive Nancy to my home, then I'm certain that William or David would be happy to bring her with their families."

"I'll drive Nancy and perhaps stay to spend the night," Mr. Geddy said quickly. "Grace is capable and will be there to assist Elizabeth."

Nancy waited for Elizabeth to agree. Grandmother waited, too, but Elizabeth busied herself with smoothing Jamie's gown and did not speak.

Jane appeared in the doorway. "Mistress Geddy, the roast and potatoes are done. Would you like me to serve the dinner?"

"Elizabeth?" Grandmother asked softly.

"Yes, thank you. I am ready for dinner," Elizabeth answered.

She didn't look toward Grandmother, Nancy noticed. She kept her eyes on Jamie. Nancy was certain that Elizabeth knew what question Grandmother had really asked her. *Will she tell me later that I can't go?* Nancy wondered. *No! Papa agreed that I could visit Grandmother, and I will remind him of his promise.*

Chapter Eight

November seemed to be an extra-busy month. Late apples, fall vegetables, and meats had to be preserved, dried, salted, or potted, and stored for use during the winter. The feather beds must be removed from the bedsteads and aired in the autumn sunshine. Grace's mattress, for her bed in the kitchen, needed to be restuffed with clean, dry straw, and clothing for the cold months ahead must be sewn, altered, and mended.

Each week, however, Nancy managed to spend one morning with the Powells, learning the receipts used for baking. And on two Sunday afternoons there were visits to Grandmother Anne's home, where fittings for Nancy's gown were made. Nancy grew more and more excited. That silky gown the color of cream would be hers to wear at her very first ball. How could she possibly wait until the Christmas season arrived?

Even though daylight hours grew shorter and they must work by candlelight, Nancy doggedly remained with her task of teaching Grace to read and write. By the last week of November Grace could print her name and identify the letters of the alphabet. She had memorized some basic words and approached each lesson with excitement.

"Soon I'll write the letter to my mother, but how will I know how to send it to her?" she asked Nancy.

"I have given this some thought," Nancy said. "Often Uncle John travels to Williamsburg from Richmond. Perhaps he knows the gentleman named Josiah Barker. If not, Uncle John could make enquiries. It shouldn't be hard to find him. Uncle John is very kind. He will deliver the letter to please me."

Grace smiled. "Could he ask how my mother does and tell me if she is well?"

"I will request that he do so," Nancy promised. She pushed the hornbook closer to Grace. "Let's get back to work," she said. "I want you to read the first line of this text."

Nancy wished that the time spent with her family

could be as peaceful as the hours she worked with Grace.

Elizabeth, pasty-faced, her hands and ankles swollen, worked at household chores so intently that she didn't try to indulge in friendly chatter. Any conversation about the current political situation was strictly forbidden.

James Geddy had no wish to discuss politics, either. But Nancy had heard, from the Powells, that the colonists were continuing to operate their businesses in defiance of the Stamp Act. Although ships were clearing colonial ports, in Virginia they sailed with certificates stating that no stamps were available in the colony. Each day Virginians were becoming more and more upset with the Crown.

Tom often seemed preoccupied as he worried about orders canceled or delayed and a noticeable drop in the number of customers at the forge.

At times, when Nancy visited Tom in the forge, he was like his former self. He diligently went about whatever job he'd been assigned to, explaining his work to Nancy or chatting easily about the farm tools or brass candleholders he was helping to create. But on a chill day near the end of November, Tom laid down the candleholder he was polishing and looked at Nancy with frightened eyes.

"If my apprenticeship should end, I'll have nowhere to go," he said.

"It won't end. It can't," Nancy said bravely. She tried to smile, hoping to reassure Tom.

"I heard Master William tell your uncle David that King George and the Parliament won't budge. Your uncles are concerned about what will happen if the Stamp Act is not soon repealed. Some of their best customers have large debt suits pending. Master William fears that soon these customers will be unable to pay for work done here at the foundry if the courts cannot meet and order payment of the debts."

Nancy heard a catch in Tom's voice as he added, "Your uncle is also concerned that Governor Fauquier will soon forbid ships to leave Virginia's harbors without stamped bills of lading. If that happens, people will not be able to send their crops to England, and so they will have no money for our services here at the foundry."

"That doesn't mean Uncle William will break his contract with you."

"It might."

Nancy put a hand on Tom's shoulder. "If the colonists stand together to oppose this tax, the king and Parliament will be bound to do away with the Stamp Tax laws."

Tom glanced toward William Geddy, who was working at the forge, hammering a bar of red-hot iron. "But they do not all stand together."

"Most of them do," Nancy quickly answered. More than ever before, Nancy wished that her father and his brothers would join their voices of protest to those of their friends.

"Have you thought of a way to persuade your father?" Tom asked.

Nancy looked down at the toes of her shoes. "I am trying," she said, "but an idea has not come to me."

Tom did not answer, so Nancy looked up into his eyes. Stung by the worry and fear she could see in them, she promised, "But I *shall* think of something, Tom. Trust me."

"Tom," Uncle William called, "I need your assistance."

"I trust you, Nancy," Tom whispered, and ran to join William Geddy.

The next day, as Nancy was on her way home from market, Harry called out to her. He waved a copy of the *Virginia Gazette* and shouted, "Wait, Nancy! I want to show you something!"

Nancy put down her heavy basket and drew her cloak more firmly around her. "Hurry," she said as

Harry skidded up to a stop in front of her. "'Tis a chill wind, and I must soon be home with my purchases."

Harry smacked the newspaper with his hand. "Joseph Royale wrote that the stamp agent in the colony of South Carolina was attacked by an angry mob."

Nancy gasped, remembering Colonel Mercer's arrival in Virginia and the anger of the men who had confronted him. "The stamp agent was not hurt, was he?"

"No. He resigned." Harry grinned. "Remember Colonel Mercer and the look on his face, like a dog afraid of a whipping?"

"He did not look like a dog afraid of a whipping, and it isn't something to laugh about," Nancy snapped.

Harry looked surprised. "Of course it is. He shouldn't have accepted the assignment. He put himself in harm's way. It was no one's fault but his."

"No matter. That doesn't give anyone the right to harm him. It's wrong!" Nancy insisted.

Frustrated, Harry slapped his leg with the newspaper. "Oh, Nancy," he said, "don't be such a . . . such a *girl*."

Angry at Harry and at King George for creating a situation that could ruin people's lives, Nancy snatched up her basket and hurried home.

She waited until after supper to talk to her father. "Papa, did you know that the stamp agent in South Carolina was forced to resign by an angry mob?" she asked. "Perhaps there will soon be an end to the Stamp Act."

James Geddy thought a moment. Then he said, "As you know, child, I was born in Scotland, less than two years before my parents emigrated to Virginia, so I've always been a loyal subject of Britain. Yet Williamsburg has long been my home, and my strongest loyalties are to Virginia."

Nancy nodded, pleased at what he had just told her and eager to hear the rest.

"To be honest with you, I am afraid of what might happen if the current policy continues. I trust that the British government will correct the wrongs it has committed against the colonies and repeal the Stamp Act." He paused, then said, "However, we must be prudent and wait to see what the king will decide."

Disturbed, since she was expecting more from her father, Nancy asked, "But if everyone does nothing but wait, will any good be done at all?"

She recognized the worry in her father's eyes as he

answered, "Prudence, child. Prudence is the only answer. Patrick Henry—who unfortunately tends to be somewhat of a firebrand—has given loud voice to our concerns in the House of Burgesses. But, to be fair, we must remember that these taxes are for our own benefit, since they will be used to pay for the defense of the colonies. We must wait until the Crown can discover the correct course to follow."

"But, Papa," Nancy complained, "won't the king be more inclined to listen to reason if *all* the men in the colonies stand together against the Stamp Act?"

"The Stamp Act Congress has sent its petition to the king," he said. "Even though no Virginians attended the congress, the petition expresses our views. Now we must let His Majesty and his ministers respond."

"What about Tom and his apprenticeship?" Nancy asked.

"I can't answer that question. It is up to your uncle William, not to me." Mr. Geddy looked questioningly at Nancy. "You have remembered your promise not to speak on the subject to your uncle, have you not?"

"Yes, Papa," Nancy answered, but she blushed. She had been seriously considering breaking this promise.

"You are a good girl, Nancy," her father said.

"Papa," Nancy wailed in desperation, "you *must* take a position on the Stamp Act."

"That is true. And when I take a position, I must be firm in it." Mr. Geddy sighed. "I'm not certain yet what I should do."

Nancy sank back in her chair. She realized nothing could be done by arguing with her father. She just wished he were a man of action. Just waiting—for any reason—didn't satisfy her. She had heard the arguments pro and con, and she'd made up her mind. The Stamp Act was wrong and must not be accepted.

Discouraged, Nancy knew that she would be unable to change her father's mind. Only other citizens, men he respected, would have any influence on his thinking. Mr. Powell, for instance . . .

"Do you have any more questions, Nancy?" her father asked.

"No, Papa," Nancy said. "I have no more questions." *But I have an idea,* she thought with growing excitement. *Oh, Tom! I think I have come up with exactly the right idea!*

As she rose from her chair Mr. Geddy said, "Lately I have seen little of you during the evenings. Elizabeth tells me that you spend a great deal of time in the kitchen."

"That's correct, Papa," Nancy said. "I am teaching Grace to read and write so that she can write a letter to her mother in Richmond."

His eyes opened wide in surprise. "That is an unusual undertaking, daughter."

Nancy rested a hand on his shoulder. "Not really, Papa," she said. "Grace has a mother who is still living. She shouldn't lose her family because they cannot hear from one another. Grace needs her mother, just as I—"

Nancy stopped abruptly. Nothing more needed to be said. Perhaps she had said too much. "Pray may I be excused now, Papa?" Nancy asked.

"Yes, you may," her father answered. He nodded encouragingly, but as Nancy glanced back from the doorway, she saw that he had slumped in his chair, resting his head in his hands.

It tore at her heart to see her father so troubled, but she had a plan to remedy that. First, she needed time to think. She had to make sure that what she wanted to do was right. Surely it would be.

Nancy remembered her father's caution to be prudent. Very well, she would be prudent. She would think her idea through, making sure it would work well. She pressed her hands to her chest, as if she could slow the quick beating of her heart. Her plan was certainly worth trying. However, if she carried it out, she could be in trouble with Elizabeth.

Nancy took a deep breath, then smiled. It didn't matter, she decided. Even if Elizabeth became angry, the results would be worth it.

Chapter Nine

On Wednesday evening during the last week of November, Nancy entered the kitchen. Grace sat at the table, bent over Nancy's copy of *Aesop's Fables*, which lay in a pool of candlelight.

Nancy flopped into a chair, leaning her elbows on the table. Elizabeth would strongly disapprove of a young lady's sitting in that position, but Nancy didn't care. "This Sunday will be the first Sunday of Advent," she said. "Grandmother is expecting visitors from Richmond, so we will not be visiting her." Nervously Nancy licked her lips before she continued. "Sunday will be a fine day to invite a small company for tea."

Grace put down the book, surprised. "Mistress Geddy wants to invite . . . ? I thought—"

"*I* wish to invite some guests to tea."

Grace looked wary as she asked, "Who do you think to invite?"

"The Powells," Nancy answered. "Mr. Powell is a friend my father greatly admires." She smiled at Grace. "I will make lemon tarts. Mrs. Powell taught me how."

"That's why you want to do this? To show Mrs. Powell you can cook?"

Nancy gave an impatient shake of her head and added, "It's important—That is, I wish to entertain the entire family, including Mr. Powell."

"Will Mistress Geddy want you to do this?"

"It will be good for her to visit with friends," Nancy said. "However, it might be best to wait until Sunday to tell her about it. I want the company to be a happy surprise."

Grace leaned back, a look of suspicion on her face. "Will we be in trouble if she's not happy?"

Nancy sighed. "*You* won't be in trouble, Grace. You will simply be doing what you've been told. *I* might be in trouble, but if I am, it won't matter. Tom needs help. Papa needs guidance. I am going to do whatever I can."

Grace looked puzzled. "I don't understand, Mistress Nancy. What has helpin' Tom and the master to do with havin' a tea?"

Nancy folded her hands together, took a few slow breaths, and smiled. "I may have confused you, since I was speaking my thoughts aloud. The tea will be a small gathering of friends. We'll serve tea and the tarts, and there will be good conversation. It will be a happy occasion."

Grace's eyebrows rose again. "You're certain Mistress Geddy will be happy, too?"

"As happy as she is able to be," Nancy said. "Will you help me with the baking, Grace?"

Grace looked down at her book and the words Nancy was teaching her to read. She smiled and raised her head. "Yes, Mistress Nancy," she said. "Tell me what you want me to do. I'll help you."

During the next few days Nancy grew more and more nervous as she thought of the many things she must do to prepare for the tea. What had she talked herself into?

There was silver to polish. The blue and white delft plates from England, which had not been in use for years, must be washed and dried. Tea would have to be measured just so for the pot, and sugar must be cut from the cone and ground until fine. The best linen napkins would need to be starched and ironed, and the tarts must be baked. All these chores had to be done without Elizabeth's knowledge.

Fortunately Elizabeth took long rests after the family's two o'clock dinners. Jamie usually napped at this time, too, so Nancy and Grace went through the tasks quickly. The linen was ironed and replaced, the silver polished and tucked back into its chest, and the washed dishes returned to their shelf. Nancy thrilled as she folded the stiff napkins and rubbed a shine into the silver spoons. She especially loved the dishes, with their cheeful blue flowers on white glaze. Nancy thought the old-fashioned plates were much prettier than the stylish brown tortoise-shell Whieldon dishes Elizabeth preferred. These beautiful things had belonged to her mother, and now she was using them—with her mother's blessing, she was certain. What did it matter what Elizabeth would think?

On Thursday morning Nancy searched Market Square for Mrs. Powell. Relieved when she found her, Nancy eagerly greeted her and her daughters.

"I'm heartily glad to see you," Nancy said. "I've an invitation to give to your family."

Quickly she told them about the tea on Sunday at five in the afternoon. Tea was usually taken at four, but Elizabeth's naps after the two o'clock dinner usually lasted until four-thirty. This would give Nancy and Grace time to set out the tea things and prepare the parlor. It would also give Elizabeth time to dress for the visitors.

"Tea?" Hannah clapped her hands. "I would love to come."

"I shall love the good things to eat," Ann said.

"The girls and I will be most happy to attend," Mrs. Powell told Nancy.

Anxiously Nancy gripped her hands together. "Mr. Powell is invited as well," she said. "Papa will be home. He will want Mr. Powell to be there, too."

"Oh," Mrs. Powell said. "Well, then, if Mr. Powell is invited, I shall accept for him. I know he'll be happy to visit in your home again."

Her smile disappeared as she studied Nancy. "Are you sure that your mother is feeling well enough to have visitors for tea?"

Nancy gulped and said, "It's a surprise for her. She hesitates to entertain because she does not feel well, but I know . . . I'm certain that she longs for the pleasure of company."

"Poor, dear Elizabeth," Mrs. Powell said. "I had not given thought to how lonely she must be."

"The tea must be a surprise," Nancy insisted. "Otherwise she will try to help and do too much."

Mrs. Powell smiled again. "We will all keep your secret, Nancy. What may I bring?"

Nancy almost groaned aloud. This tea was growing out of hand. "Please don't bring anything," she said. "It's to be very simple fare—just tea and the lemon tarts you taught me to bake."

Mrs. Powell thought a moment. "It will be hard to bake the tarts at your home without Elizabeth wondering why. Suppose, instead of our baking lesson this morning, you come on Saturday. We'll bake the treats then."

"Wonderful!" Nancy cried. She stretched out her arms to hug Mrs. Powell, Hannah, and Ann at the same time. "This will be exactly what I hoped for!"

Nancy worked so hard on preparations for the tea that Saturday arrived quickly. After breakfast she dropped the leaves of the dining room table and placed the chairs against the wall.

Tomorrow is the tea, and Elizabeth doesn't suspect a thing, she thought with delight.

Soon Elizabeth would tuck Jamie into his trundle bed for a nap, then probably lie down to rest herself. Grace was prepared to keep Jamie busy after he awoke, while Nancy hurried over to the Powells' to bake the lemon tarts.

Elizabeth spoke from the doorway. "Nancy, I've asked Grace to take care of Jamie," she said.

Nancy gave a guilty jump, afraid that Elizabeth had read her thoughts.

"I realize that you didn't go to the Powells' for a baking lesson this week," Elizabeth said. "So I decided that this morning would be a perfect time in which to teach you to bake my mother's queen's cake."

"Oh!" Nancy cried out without thinking. "I can't!"

"Why can't you?" Elizabeth looked bewildered.

"Mrs. Powell changed our lesson from Thursday to Saturday this week. I—I'm sorry I didn't tell you."

Elizabeth's voice was low but firm. "Oh? What will you be learning to bake?"

"Lemon tarts," Nancy answered quickly.

"I believe you learned to make lemon tarts a few weeks ago. You brought some home to share with us."

Elizabeth's doubt showed on her face, and Nancy's back stiffened. Why should she have to explain to Elizabeth what she was doing? She matched Elizabeth's tone as she said, "As I remember, you said that the bottom crusts were soggy. I'm following the proverb 'Practice makes perfect.' "

Elizabeth sighed. Nancy could see the pain in her eyes. "I had hoped . . . that is, if you and I were to work together, then perhaps . . ." She didn't finish the statement.

Guilt filled Nancy as she looked at her stepmother. She hadn't meant to hurt Elizabeth, but it was obvious that she had. Elizabeth was trying to be kind by sharing her own mother's receipt, Nancy knew, and in turn she should graciously accept the lesson. But she couldn't. Not this morning. How could she make Elizabeth understand?

"I would love to learn how to make your mother's queen's cake," Nancy said politely, "but some other time. I promised Mrs. Powell I would come. She'll be waiting for me."

"I see," Elizabeth said quietly.

Nancy was terrified that Elizabeth would refuse to allow her to go to the Powells' and her plans would be ruined. They couldn't be. Papa had to be set on the right footing, and—given time to explain his position—Mr. Powell could do it. "I really do want to learn to make your mother's queen's cake," Nancy insisted. "But I can't today. Please understand."

"I do understand," Elizabeth said quietly. She turned and left the room.

Nancy plopped into one of the chairs, stifling a groan. Elizabeth sincerely had wanted to share time with her, and in turn Nancy had hurt Elizabeth's feelings. But what choice did she have? She couldn't tell Elizabeth about the company ahead of time, or her plans might be canceled.

"What shall I do?" Nancy whispered aloud. "What in the world shall I do?"

When no answer came to mind, she sighed. What else could she do but go on with her plans? The company would arrive tomorrow afternoon at five o'clock. Papa would be strongly influenced to join the other men of Williamsburg in refusing to accept the Stamp Act, and Elizabeth would see how wrong she was to decline to host Christmas-season dinners in their home.

The tea would be a happy occasion, and it would have a happy ending—just as Nancy had planned.

Or would it?

Chapter Ten

On Sunday afternoon Nancy helped Grace spruce up the dining room and kitchen. Then, hands trembling with excitement, Nancy took out the delftware, the silver teaspoons, and the napkins.

She had forgotten that on Sunday afternoons, while Elizabeth and Jamie napped, Papa always sat in his favorite chair in the parlor and read passages from the Bible. However, she knew that if she was patient enough, his eyes would close and he'd sleep soundly in his chair. Then she could quietly prepare the room.

Before Grace hurried to the Powells' house to get the lemon tarts, Nancy warned her, "Do not run while you are carrying the tarts. Watch where you step. Whatever you do, Grace, don't drop the tarts."

"Yes, Mistress Nancy," Grace answered. She ran in the direction of the Powells' home.

Nancy hoped for the best. The moment her father fell asleep, she began arranging the parlor.

Accompanied by her father's light snores, Nancy brought in the linens and tea wares. When she had finished she stood back and clasped her hands together in admiration. The parlor was cheerful and bright, but not too festive, as befitted the solemnity of Advent. It was an inviting room in which Mr. Powell would relax and enjoy speaking his political views. As for Elizabeth, she would have no work to do and could only benefit by the friendly concern of Mrs. Powell.

"What have you done to the parlor, Nancy? What is taking place?" Elizabeth spoke sharply.

Her heart beating rapidly, Nancy whirled to face her stepmother.

Startled, Mr. Geddy struggled from sleep, sitting upright. "What is wrong, madam?" he managed to ask. "Why are you frowning?"

Elizabeth strode into the room and pointed at the tea things that had been set out. "I simply asked what *this* is all about," she said.

Nancy's father stared at the delftware and silver. "I have no idea," he answered in bewilderment.

Nancy tried not to let her voice give away her nervousness. "The Powell family is coming to tea today at five," she said.

Elizabeth's mouth fell open. "Not here. Not today."

Nancy nodded eagerly. "Yes, today."

"But they were not invited."

"I invited them," Nancy said. She looked at her father's prized clock, which rested on a nearby table. "I made lemon tarts, Grace and I readied the napkins, silver, and delftware, and I planned to waken you soon so that you could change your gown."

Elizabeth's lips parted and she looked as if she was about to speak, so Nancy quickly added, "This is an opportunity for you and Papa to have a pleasant visit with friends. Grace and I will clean up afterward. There are no chores for you to do."

Elizabeth smiled, although her eyes filled with tears. "Nancy dear," she said, "now I understand why yesterday you were so insistent about going to the Powells' home. This was a wonderfully kind thing for you to do." Resting a hand on Nancy's shoulder, Elizabeth added, "As you pointed out, I have had none of the work in the preparations and need only relax and enjoy the tea."

Mr. Geddy chuckled. "And I, for one, look forward to a good visit with Benjamin and Annabelle Powell."

He put an arm around Elizabeth's shoulders and walked with her toward their bedchamber. "Let us find a pretty gown for you to wear," he said.

Nancy leaned against the wall, stunned at Elizabeth's happiness. Nancy should have felt happy, too, but instead her chest felt tight and miserable with guilt. Both Papa and Elizabeth thought that Nancy had planned this as a gift for Elizabeth. They didn't know her real reason for hosting the tea.

There is no need for them to know, she cautioned herself. Yet she felt even more guilty that she should be given credit for reaching out to Elizabeth with a kindness she hadn't truly meant.

Grace, gingerly carrying a large basket, hurried into the parlor. "Here are the lemon tarts," she said.

At least the tarts have arrived safely. 'Tis a good omen, Nancy thought.

By the time the Powells arrived, Elizabeth had changed to a new gown and cap. Nancy still wore the gown and cap she had worn to church but had washed her face. Little Jamie was well scrubbed and wore a clean white gown. Mr. Geddy greeted the visitors with warmth and led them into the parlor.

Hannah greeted Mr. and Mrs. Geddy with a polite

curtsey. Then she hugged Nancy. "I love teas," she whispered.

As the guests were being seated, it was difficult for Nancy to decide who beamed at her with more pride and approval, her father or Mrs. Powell. Guilt made it hard for her to meet their eyes. Nancy knew they both thought she had planned the gathering as a favor to Elizabeth, and she had let them believe that was true. But what else was she to do? She couldn't tell them that she wanted the tea only so Mr. Powell would air his political beliefs and influence her father.

As soon as she had poured the tea into tea bowls, passing them, with Hannah's help, to all the guests, Nancy cleared her throat. "Mr. Powell," she said, "I've heard that you have expressed some excellent and forceful opinions on the effects of the Stamp Act."

"Thank you, Nancy." Mr. Powell gave a little bow, but Mrs. Powell interrupted, placing a hand on his arm.

" 'Tis certainly true that Mr. Powell has some forceful opinions," she said as she smiled at her husband. "But he has promised me there will be no political talk today. We are here to celebrate good friendship and enjoy a pleasant afternoon."

"But we *want* to hear Mr. Powell's ideas. We would enjoy hearing them," Nancy insisted.

"Nancy, dear, you are a considerate hostess." Mrs. Powell waggled a finger and laughed. "But my dear husband has promised me."

She leaned toward Elizabeth. "Are you in need of an extra baby quilt?" she asked. "I have a soft white wool flannel one, with lovely blue blanket stitching on the edges, and . . ." She and Elizabeth were soon engrossed in talk about their children.

Nancy busied herself serving the lemon tarts while she tried to think of what to do next.

"Yum!" Ann murmured, biting into her tart after Nancy had made the rounds. "I hope there are plenty of tarts. One might not be enough. Two would be better."

Two would be better? With a suddenly light heart Nancy smiled at Ann. "Of course two would be better," she said. "Please excuse me while I add more water to the kettle."

She took the kettle from its fireplace hook and hurried outside to the kitchen. "Grace," she called out, "will you take a message to Master John Greenhow across the street? Tell him, please, that the Powells have stopped by for lemon tarts, and we would like him and his children to come, too."

Grace eyed the tarts remaining in the basket. "Good thing you made plenty."

"Yes, it is," Nancy said. She was filled with excitement. Mr. Greenhow hadn't promised not to speak about the effects of the Stamp Act. With the small children in the house distracting the women, and two of the men hoping to turn the third over to their way of thinking, the conversation she longed for was bound to take place.

Nancy returned to the parlor with a full teakettle, smiling when a few moments later there was a knock at the front door.

As she had guessed, the young Greenhow children played happily in the dining room with Jamie. The two women busied themselves keeping an eye on the children, chatting about the care of babies and growing children, and the latest fashions. In the parlor, Mr. Greenhow and Mr. Powell began pointing out the need for a solid front in rebelling against the Stamp Act.

"We must manage our businesses as well as we can until the king makes his decision," Nancy heard her father say as she entered the parlor to offer more tea.

"Of course," Mr. Greenhow told him. "However, we can help the king and Parliament come to their senses if we all stand together and refuse to pay the taxes."

Mr. Geddy showed his indecision. "The taxes are wrong, yes, but—"

"We must present a solid front, James."

"My brothers and I—"

"Have you spoken about this to your brother David? Only yesterday he agreed with me on our position."

"He did?" Mr. Geddy was surprised. "And William?"

"If David takes a stand, I believe that William will as well. Join us, James."

Nancy held her breath. She knew that Hannah was speaking to her, but she couldn't listen. She must hear what her father had to say.

But as the clock chimed, Mrs. Powell appeared in the passage. "Look at the time," she said. "We've been having such a lovely visit, I'm sure we've overstayed our welcome."

There were praises for Nancy's tarts and for the agreeable time they had all had. Mrs. Powell promised to call on Elizabeth soon and bring her the baby quilt.

As the men shook hands Mr. Powell said to Mr. Geddy, "Think about what we've told you, James. We need your support."

Nancy twisted her fingers together, waiting for her father's answer.

"I'll give it serious thought, Ben," he said.

Although Nancy had been hoping that her father would be quickly won over, she was content to know that he had been given some good arguments to think about. He was a fair and just man, and he was a loyal Virginian. He had told her so, and she knew it was true.

As the door closed on the last of the guests, Mr. Geddy smiled at Nancy. "It was good to entertain old friends again," he said.

Elizabeth turned to Nancy. "All the guests seem to have enjoyed themselves," she said, "and I did as well. The tea was a lovely surprise.

"And by the way, child," Elizabeth added, "your tarts were very good. You had ground the sugar well, so there were no lumps, and the bottom crusts were not soggy."

"I thank you," Nancy murmured, and hurried toward the doorway. The lump of guilt that rose in her throat made it hard to speak. It was time now to tell Tom what she had done. They would have to wait to see if Mr. Powell and Mr. Greenhow had influenced her father, but Nancy had heard what they said. Their arguments had been good, and she had hopes.

In any case, the tea had been a success.

Chapter Eleven

On Monday evening Nancy returned to her task of teaching Grace to read and write.

Making few errors, Grace slowly read aloud a story from *Aesop's Fables,* and Nancy smiled.

"I think it's time for you to write your letter to your mother," she said.

Grace's eyes widened, and her hands trembled. "Already? Oh, Mistress Nancy, I don't think I can."

"Of course you can. I'll help you with the words you don't know."

Tears began to roll down Grace's cheeks. "Mistress Nancy, I ain't seen my mother for three years. I don't know what to say to her in a letter."

Nancy leaned across the table. "Grace," she said,

"you have a mother you can write to. I . . . not everybody does. What did you say to her when you were with her? You can say that now."

"I'm not the same now. I'm near grown. I was just a child when I was with my mother. At times I try to remember her face . . . and I can't." Grace's voice dropped to a whisper. "At night I would snuggle down next to her on her pallet. She'd put her arms around me, and sometimes she'd sing to me. Her breath was warm against my forehead, and no matter how tired I was I wanted us to go on like that forever and ever."

Nancy swallowed hard and rubbed at her own eyes. "Grace, I will get a quill pen, inkwell, penknife, pounce, sealing wax, and seal, and a sheet of Papa's paper. While I'm gathering them, you think about what you would like your mother to know about you." She rose from her chair, adding, "I'll be right back."

By the time Nancy returned, Grace had dried her eyes. But when Grace picked up the quill pen her fingers still shook.

Cautiously Nancy steadied the inkwell. Then she pointed to the paper. "Write the date up here. Write 'December sixteenth, 1765.' "

She watched as Grace laboriously dipped the quill

point into the ink and printed the words and numbers. Then Nancy picked up the slate pencil and slate and asked, "What do you want to write?"

"I want to tell her about you and Master and Mistress Geddy and Jamie, of course, so she'll know I'm treated well. And I should tell her how she can find me and ask if there's anyone can write a letter for her to send to me."

Nancy nodded, but Grace went on, "I want to tell my mother in this letter that I love her just like we was still together. Just like her arms were still around me. Can I do that?"

"Yes," Nancy said. "Your mother would like that."

Grace dictated to Nancy, who wrote the sentences on the slate. Carefully Grace dipped her quill pen in the ink. She slowly copied the sentences, then dictated more. Finally Grace finished her letter.

After the ink had dried, Nancy folded the sheet so that Grace's writing was on the inside. She turned the folded letter over and wrote the Geddys' address and "Williamsburg, Virginia," in the top left-hand corner. "What's your mother's name?" Nancy asked, surprised that she hadn't thought of asking before.

"Lettice," Grace said.

Nancy wrote "To Lettice, in care of Mr. and Mrs. Josiah Barker of Richmond, Virginia" on the folded paper. She turned the letter over, put the tip of the stick of red sealing wax into the candle flame, then pressed the softened end where the paper opened. She pressed the seal into the drop of wax. Now the letter would remain closed until Grace's mother broke the seal.

"I will see Uncle John on Sunday at Grandmother's house," she told Grace. "I'll ask him to deliver the letter, and he will."

Grace stood and faced Nancy, but it seemed to take a great deal of effort before she was able to speak. A tear rolled down her cheek. "I thank you, Mistress Nancy," she whispered.

"Oh, Grace!" Nancy said, folding her in a hug. She didn't try to wipe away her own tears.

On Sunday Grandmother Anne said, "You can't imagine how eagerly I'm looking forward to having you with me, Nancy." Her smile broadened as she added, "Your gown is finished and laid on my bed. Why don't you try it on and show us how it looks?"

Nancy ran to the bedchamber and held up the gown. It was even more beautiful now that all the trimmings were in place. With the help of Meg, one of Grandmother's house slaves, Nancy tried on the gown and its matching petticoat.

Returning to the parlor, Nancy modeled the gown. She turned full circle so Papa and Grandmother could see the lace flounces on the three-quarter-length sleeves, the fitted bodice in front, and the pleats falling loosely from her shoulders in back.

"Dear child," Mr. Geddy said, "you look so like—" He stopped speaking, cleared his throat, and added, "The cream color of the gown sets off your hair and eyes perfectly."

"'Tis lovely! The gown is perfect for you," Grandmother exclaimed. She leaned back in her chair, looking pleased with herself.

Elizabeth said nothing.

Surely she won't try to stop my visit at the last minute by insisting she needs me, Nancy reassured herself. However, as she glanced at her stepmother a cold trickle of worry shivered down her spine.

When John Geddy arrived, Nancy gave him the letter and explained how and why Grace had written it.

Uncle John smiled. "As it happens, my dear niece, I am acquainted with Mr. Josiah Barker in Richmond. I will be most heartily glad to stop by his home and deliver the letter to his slave Lettice, since this will please you."

"Thank you, Uncle John," Nancy said.

Her uncle nodded. "Do you know there are two schools of thought in regard to teaching slaves to read and write?"

Nancy shook her head, puzzled. "I have heard that Mrs. Wager's school was founded by church officials to teach very young slaves to read their catechism so that they would understand their religion. Is that what you mean?"

"There are many slave owners in Virginia who believe that reading and writing are skills that make their slaves more valuable," Uncle John explained. "But there is some feeling—especially in the Carolinas—that it is dangerous to give slaves any form of education. The power of knowing how to read and write could foment a desire for independence and a longing to rebel or run away."

"Grace wouldn't rebel. She wouldn't run away," Nancy insisted.

Uncle John put an arm around Nancy's shoulders and gave her a light hug. "Child, you were motivated by the kindness in your own heart, but you did not stop to ask yourself what good would come of Grace writing to her mother.

"The Barkers are elderly, and I have heard that Josiah Barker is not in the best of health. When he departs this life, his property, including his slaves, will be divided among his widow and their children. One son lives in Bedford County and the other in Mecklenburg County. Grace will not see her mother again. Is it not best to let her forget her mother and her childhood so that she may concentrate on her work and become content?"

Nancy looked steadily at her uncle. "I was with my mother only as an infant, much too young for memories, and I ache to remember her."

Uncle John patted Nancy's shoulder. "Nancy, dear, I apologize. For a few moments I forgot what it is like to view the world through the innocent eyes of a child." He stepped back and gave a little bow. "Believe me, I will gladly deliver Grace's letter with much pleasure."

"Thank you, Uncle John," Nancy answered. But as she walked out to the garden behind Grandmother's house, she puzzled over all that her uncle had said. If children clearly could understand the pain of separation from a dearly loved mother, then why was it so impossible for adults to understand?

Chapter Twelve

On Christmas day the air was cold but golden with sun. Nancy dressed quickly and hurried to set up the table and chairs for breakfast. In honor of the day she used the delftware, the table silver, and their best linen napkins and cloth.

Jamie, in his wrinkled nightwear, ran into the room laughing. He flung himself at Nancy, hugging her around the legs.

Nancy picked him up, first checking the state of his clout. It was clean and fresh, which meant Elizabeth and Papa were awake and up, too.

Suddenly Jamie clung to Nancy as the sounds of gunfire echoed outside. "Don't be frightened," she told him. "It's only the men in town shooting their guns to announce that it's Christmas."

"Chrismis?" Jamie asked.

Nancy laughed. She swung him up and down until he squealed. "Christmas is the birthday of the infant Jesus."

"Birfday?" Jamie echoed.

Nancy laughed again, nuzzling the baby fat on his neck. "Come with me," she said. "We'll help Grace in the kitchen. I'm already hungry for breakfast."

Close to eight o'clock the family was seated around the table. As Grace brought a plate of sliced bread to the table, Mr. Geddy rose and handed something to her.

Nancy knew that her father usually gave Grace a coin for Christmas. She had wondered whether his concerns about his business and the effects of the Stamp Act would prevent him from giving her one this year. But Grace reacted so happily, Nancy knew her father's gift had been generous.

"Oh, thank you, Master Geddy!" Grace cried. She turned quickly and ran back outside to the kitchen.

Mr. Geddy smiled at Nancy. "I believe you have been hoping to buy a ribbon to wear with your new dress. I am certain John Greenhow will have one the right color."

He placed a silver wedge in Nancy's hand. On it she saw half of a shield and crown, worn numbers, and letters. "It is half of a Spanish two-reales coin that I received from a customer," Mr. Geddy explained.

Nancy was sure that when Mr. Greenhow weighed the two-reales piece, it would buy enough ribbon to tie around her neck and decorate her cap. "Thank you, Papa!" she said.

Mr. Geddy turned to Elizabeth. "Madam, may I give you Jamie's gift for safekeeping?" he asked.

"Pretty!" Jamie cried. He tried to reach his half of the small silver two-reales coin, which his mother put into her pocket.

"There is one more gift, if you will excuse me but a moment," he said.

When he returned to the dining room, he placed a pair of mitts on the table in front of Elizabeth. They were the most beautiful ones Nancy had ever seen, made of white ribbed silk with blue embroidery. As Elizabeth picked up one of the mitts and turned it over, Nancy saw that the point was lined with blue silk and the rest with cream leather.

"I hope they please you, madam," Mr. Geddy said. "Your old mitts have worn thin, and I know how much discomfort the cold causes you. You should be comfortable, especially when you already feel unwell." He smiled at Elizabeth so tenderly that Nancy looked away.

Elizabeth's voice was small. "I have nowhere to wear them. Since we will not entertain this season—"

Mr. Geddy interrupted. "You can wear them to church services this noon," he said.

Hurt by the disappointed note in her father's voice, Nancy quickly spoke up. "You will look lovely," she said to Elizabeth. "Every woman will wish she had such beautiful mitts."

"That is not a modest wish," Elizabeth said. Pink spotted her cheeks as she blushed in embarrassment. "My wish is to be unobtrusive. I do *not* wish to be the center of all eyes."

Nancy wanted to tell Elizabeth she was ruining her father's gift, but Elizabeth's face was so tight with misery, Nancy could only try to draw attention away from her.

"Papa," Nancy said loudly, "I cannot wait to select my ribbon. May I go to Mr. Greenhow's store as soon as it opens tomorrow and finish my chores afterward?"

Nancy saw Elizabeth look up as if to say something, but her father answered first. "Of course you may."

"Thank you, Papa!" Nancy shoved back her chair and leaped to her feet. She ran to her father's chair and hugged him.

As her father hugged her in return, Elizabeth said, "Grace has brought in the milk hominy. Pray sit down, Nancy, so your father may serve us."

Nancy hurried to her chair. Not even Elizabeth could dampen her spirits today. She couldn't wait to take her gift to church to show Hannah and Ann.

Mr. Geddy smiled broadly as he began to fill each plate. "The Christmas season was always the happiest time of the year for me when I was a boy," he said. "After church services we'd hang holly sprays in each window and tie a few sprigs of mistletoe together to dangle from the ceiling. Mother would create a feast of roast goose, turkey, ham, fish, and oysters, and there were always mincemeat pies, a plum pudding, and brandied fruit."

"And your father would give the children and slaves their gifts," Nancy added.

"Not on Christmas day," Mr. Geddy said. "Papa

kept to the old custom of presenting gifts on Twelfth Night—the feast of the Epiphany."

Nancy gently stroked the two-reales half, which she had laid beside her plate. "I'm glad you give your gifts on Christmas day," she said.

Later, before the services began, Nancy ran to meet her friends. She pulled Papa's gift from her pocket. "Look!" she said.

Hannah and Ann squealed. "Oh!" Hannah cried. "What will you buy with it?"

"Ribbon to match my gown," Nancy answered.

"Lovely!" Hannah sighed dreamily.

But Ann said, "I wish Papa gave us our gifts on Christmas day instead of New Year's."

Hannah sighed and said, "And I wish Papa would talk of something other than the Stamp Act during the twelve days of Christmas."

As more parishioners arrived in the churchyard, Nancy discovered that the Stamp Act was casting a shadow over Christmas for many of them, too. People were still concerned about what would happen if the act remained in force.

Nancy heard more conversations about the hated Stamp Act than about any dinners, visits, or weddings that would occur during the twelve days of Christmas. Even the town's leading citizens spoke little of the holiday balls they would be hosting and attending.

Tom arrived with the William Geddy family. His smile was so broad that Nancy knew Uncle William had given him a generous gift.

The bells suddenly rang, their notes so joyful that Nancy eagerly entered Bruton Parish Church.

The altar was decorated with holly and ivy. Polished wood gleamed in the early-afternoon sunlight. And Mr. Pelham, the organist, played a selection so joyful Nancy was sure it must have been written by Handel.

As the Reverend Mr. Horrocks entered the chancel Nancy made a solemn promise to herself to concentrate on her prayers. But his sermon was long, and she couldn't help thinking ahead to her four days with Grandmother. This was going to be the best Christmas season ever.

Nancy glanced down the pew at her family members. Papa—so serious as he listened intently to the sermon—was such a kind, good father. Jamie, half asleep on his mother's lap, looked more like a Christmas angel than a mischievous little boy. And Elizabeth . . . She was not wearing the mitts, even though her husband had asked her to. Nancy felt a wave of fury at her stubborn stepmother.

Elizabeth, who seemed to sense that Nancy was glaring at her, frowned and gave a slight nod toward the pulpit. Nancy knew what that meant: *Pay attention to what the rector is saying.*

Resentfully Nancy looked up at the pulpit. Her joyful mood was gone. *I will not think about Elizabeth,* she promised herself. *I will not. I will not.*

Later, as the Geddys returned to their home, Elizabeth drew Nancy aside, out of Mr. Geddy's hearing. "Put your gift in a safe place," she said. "It was meant to be used to purchase ribbon, not to show your friends before church services. You might have lost your father's generous gift. If you had, you would not be able to buy your ribbon, and that would disappoint your father. When you are given something valuable, you must take better care of it."

Nancy felt as if whatever was inside her, holding her together, had suddenly burst. All the angry feelings she had for Elizabeth came spilling out.

"*I* disappoint Papa? I pleased him by telling him how much I liked my Christmas gift. 'Tis more than I can say for you," she cried. "The mitts are beautiful, and he asked you to wear them. You were ungrateful about the gift, and you cared nothing for how happy he would be if you wore the mitts."

Elizabeth gasped and backed up a step. "The mitts were not appropriate," she began. "'Twas best that—"

Nancy didn't let her finish the sentence. "Of course they were appropriate. Besides, they were a gift. A gift should be received graciously. Aren't you always trying to tell *me* how to behave? Well, *you* should learn good behavior, too."

The words poured out, and she couldn't stop them. "And you should try harder to make a happy home for Papa. You complain you feel ill. Perhaps if you decorated the house with greenery in the windowpanes, making it a cheerful place, and invited his friends to a dinner or two, you would feel better, because you wouldn't be thinking only of yourself. You heard him tell us how much he loved the holidays in his boyhood. If you were to make our house just as cheerful, you'd be doing something Papa would enjoy."

"Enough, Nancy," Elizabeth said sternly.

"Remember how happy Papa was at the tea I gave? He likes entertaining his friends in his home. Can't you see this?"

Elizabeth's voice rose. "Nancy! You have said enough!"

Nancy was surprised by her own outburst. It was easy to see that Elizabeth was shocked, too, and hurt. Nancy shuddered at what she had boldly told her stepmother. No doubt Elizabeth would tell Papa. Perhaps she'd be forbidden to go to Grandmother's as a punishment.

Nancy knew she should apologize to Elizabeth, but she couldn't. She wouldn't!

Confused and miserable, Nancy turned and fled to her bedchamber.

Chapter Thirteen

The argument left a rough, gaping hole that needed to be filled. Nancy still felt bad about hurting Elizabeth's feelings and wanted to apologize for her outburst, but she couldn't. Over and over she told herself that the argument was Elizabeth's fault, too. Was it not? Elizabeth had said unkind things as well.

There was no understanding Elizabeth's behavior. There were times in which she seemed to be offering her friendship. But just when Nancy thought she might even begin to like Elizabeth, her stepmother became stern or overly critical.

I will be traveling to Grandmother's house the day after tomorrow, Nancy reminded herself. *I should not leave without making amends.* But what she had told

Elizabeth had been the truth, and there was nothing further she could say. It would be wrong to tell Elizabeth that she hadn't meant her blunt words. Nancy felt an immense relief that she would soon be away from home. Grandmother's house would be festive and happy.

On Friday morning, as Nancy began to tidy the dining room after breakfast, James Geddy remarked that recent sales in his shop had been better than he'd expected, despite people's concerns about the effects of the Stamp Act.

Nancy put down the chair she was placing against the wall and faced her father. "What about the customers who refused to buy wares from you and your brothers?" she blurted out.

Mr. Geddy looked startled. "What do you mean?"

"I mean your former customers who would not bring their business to you because you and Uncle William and Uncle David did not join in the protest against the Stamp Act. I overheard Mrs. Gooseley say that you may lose customers and the foundry could be in trouble."

Shaking his head, Mr. Geddy said, "Mrs. Gooseley is a known gossip, Nancy. She makes up tales to suit her fancy. You cannot believe anything the woman says."

"But Tom told me that orders had been canceled

131

and not as many customers were coming to the forge or to your shop."

"Tom was right," Mr. Geddy explained. "But that was only because people became cautious in their business dealings, fearing the problems the Stamp Act might bring."

Nancy gave a long sigh of relief. "Then Uncle William won't have to let Tom go."

"Don't worry about Tom," Mr. Geddy said. "He will not be deserted. David has offered his support if necessary. I can be counted on, too."

He smiled. "On Thursday of last week your uncles, William and David, and I met with John Greenhow and Benjamin Powell. We decided to follow Mr. Greenhow's and Mr. Powell's example and stand united in protest against the Stamp Act. We are now convinced that our primary allegiance is with Virginia, not with King George, and we cannot quietly accept these new taxes."

Nancy gasped. Her plan had worked. There was no doubt her tea had been a success. "Papa! You have taken the right position," she said.

His smile grew broader. "How does a young lady become an expert on political affairs?"

"Oh, Papa." Nancy laughed and hugged her father's arm. "Young ladies can think, too."

"I was certain young ladies thought only of balls and the latest of fashions," he teased.

Nancy had achieved what she had wanted. Troubles with the Crown would not affect the foundry. She quickly finished her chore, threw on her cloak, and raced out to the forge.

"Tom!" she cried. "I have heard from Papa that he and Uncle William and Uncle David have joined those who are protesting the Stamp Act. There has been no plan for people not to buy from the Geddys. In fact, sales have gone up. And you will remain in your apprenticeship."

She savored the surprise, relief, and joy that passed over Tom's face. "My plan worked," she said quietly. "Mr. Powell and Mr. Greenhow were able to influence my father when they came to our house for tea."

Tom grinned. "Nancy, what you accomplished was the best Christmas gift I have ever been given."

Nancy felt her cheeks grow warm as she smiled back at Tom. She could not imagine a happier Christmas season.

The decorations in Grandmother's house looked very much as Papa had described them. Sprigs of holly were in all the windows, and mistletoe hung from the dining room ceiling.

Throughout the day other family members arrived. Grandmother's slaves worked diligently to set chairs around the perimeter of the room that would be turned into a ballroom. Grandmother's huge punch bowl was placed on one table, along with her best cups, plates, forks, and napkins. Nancy had tried to peek into the outdoor kitchen but had been chased away by people too busy assembling the garnishes for the custards, tarts, mince pies, and puddings that would be served.

Uncle John arrived at the same time as Uncle William and his family. Amid the noise of the many greetings, Uncle John motioned to Nancy to follow him to a back room. There he reached inside his waistcoat, removed a letter, and handed it to Nancy.

" 'Tis the letter Grace wrote to her mother," Nancy said in surprise. "Were you unable to deliver it?"

"The slave, Lettice, now lives with Mr. Barker's son George in Bedford County in western Virginia," Uncle John said.

Nancy looked up in bewilderment. "Couldn't Mr. Barker send the letter on to his son to give to Lettice?"

Uncle John put a hand on Nancy's shoulder. "I'm

sorry, child. He didn't wish to do so. He felt it would cause unwelcome feelings in Lettice and distract her from her work."

Angrily Nancy blurted out, "It was not *his* letter. He had no right to make such a decision."

"On the contrary," Uncle John said. "He had every right. Lettice is his property." He put a comforting arm around Nancy's shoulders. "Your intentions were only the best, and that's what counts."

Nancy had already begun to make plans. No matter what Mr. Barker thought, Lettice would be greatly pleased to hear from Grace. Lettice was now with a Mr. George Barker in Bedford Country, so Nancy knew how to find her. It might take time, and she'd have to work to convince Grace not to give in to discouragement.

A fiddler arrived and began tuning his fiddle. Nancy knew that later Uncle William might bring out his own fiddle, and that the two fiddles would provide music for the dance. She could hardly wait for the ball to begin.

Finally, as it was beginning to grow dark, Nancy washed in the basin with the warm water Meg had brought. She put on the beautiful gown, trying to hold still while Meg pinned the stomacher in place.

Meg swept up Nancy's hair, pinning the curls and

some of Nancy's ribbon on top of her head. Finally Meg tied another piece of ribbon around Nancy's neck. She stepped back and smiled. "Now you are ready to greet your grandmother's guests," she said.

Nancy took a quick glance in the looking glass on Grandmother's dressing table. With her hair pinned up she seemed much older. Her cheeks were pink, and her eyes sparkled with excitment. "Thank you, Meg," Nancy said.

As she opened the door of the bedchamber she heard music. Eager for the ball to begin, she hurried downstairs.

Shadows were softened by the golden glow of candle-light, and the air was fragrant with cinnamon and cedar. Flames in the wide fireplace burned brightly, and the polished wooden chairs and tables gleamed.

Some of Grandmother's neighbors began to arrive, and Nancy greeted each of them, taking special delight in those who were near her own age.

She was surprised to see Harry Armistead and his grandmother, Mrs. Wetherburn, arrive with one of the neighbors.

Harry stared at her, his mouth open. "Is that really you, Nancy?" he asked.

"Of course it's me," Nancy answered with a giggle.

Harry stepped closer. "I'm glad you're here," he

said. "My grandmother said I'd have to dance with girls. You're a girl, so if I'm with you, my grandmother will probably leave me alone."

Nancy stared at Harry. "Are you asking me for a dance?"

"Well . . . uh . . . ," Harry began.

At that moment one of Nancy's cousins arrived with a friend, Charles Pelham, the son of the Bruton Parish organist. Nancy looked up into seventeen-year-old Charles's eyes. He smiled, and she smiled back.

She turned to Harry. "Ask me later," Nancy said. "Who knows? I may have one dance not spoken for."

"Nancy!" Harry complained. "I thought you would rescue me."

"Not tonight," Nancy said.

As the fiddlers tuned their instruments and couples took their places in the center of the room, Charles Pelham appeared at Nancy's side. With a slight bow he held out an arm to Nancy. "May I—"

The front door burst open, and John Greenhow strode through the passage and into the dining room. He hadn't dressed for a ball. His cloak was askew, and he'd forgotten his gloves. He quickly bent over Grandmother's outstretched hand before he turned to James Geddy.

"James!" he cried. "You're needed at home. Elizabeth fell from a ladder."

Nancy gasped, and Grandmother cried, "The baby!"

Mr. Greenhow shook his head. "Catherine Blaikley came immediately. She said no harm was done to the child. It's Elizabeth who was hurt. She has sprained an ankle. Katherine wrapped it tightly and told her to stay off her feet for at least two weeks."

Mr. Geddy frowned in worry. "Thank you, John, for bringing the news. I'll return home right away."

For a moment Nancy hesitated. Then she took a deep breath and stepped forward. "I'll go with you, Papa," she said.

Grandmother looked as unhappy as Nancy felt. "Nancy, dear. You need not go. Grace is there to help."

"Grace should not have allowed Elizabeth to climb on a ladder," Nancy said firmly. "I must go home, Grandmother. Elizabeth will need more care than Grace can give her."

And Grace will need care, too, Nancy thought, as she remembered the returned letter.

Suddenly Nancy realized all that Mr. Greenhow had said. She asked him, "Why was Elizabeth on a ladder?"

"She had been cutting ivy. She told me she was decorating the house for you and your father."

Nancy forced back a sob as she hugged her grandmother. It pained her to leave, but it pained her even more to think of Elizabeth, home alone. In her own way, she had been trying to be a good wife and mother. To her surprise, Nancy felt a real burst of affection for her and wanted to care for her.

"Thank you for inviting me to your ball and asking me to stay a few days," she said. "I love my gown. I love *you*, Grandmother."

"You are a good girl, Nancy," Grandmother said as she helped her with her cloak. "I'm proud of you."

Nancy didn't feel proud of herself. All the way home, perched next to her father's saddle on the riding chair, she agonized over what she had said to Elizabeth and what Elizabeth must have been feeling. *I'll try to make it up to her,* Nancy promised herself.

Nancy didn't speak on the ride home, but neither did her father. She knew they were both lost in thoughts of their own.

When they arrived home, Tom ran out to put away the chair and care for the horse. With just a quick greeting to Tom, Nancy ran past him and into the house.

Grace met them at the door. "Mistress Geddy's

asleep," she whispered, but Mr. Geddy simply nodded and quietly strode to his and Elizabeth's bedchamber.

Nancy threw off her cloak. As Grace took it Nancy said, "I'm sorry, Grace. Uncle John couldn't deliver the letter you wrote to your mother. She now lives with Mr. Barker's son George in western Virginia."

Grace's eyes widened in surprise. "Couldn't Mr. Barker send the letter on to where his son lives?"

Nancy swallowed hard. How could she tell Grace why Mr. Barker refused to do so? She thought a moment, then said, "Mr. Barker is very old, Grace. He does not think as we do. He was afraid that the letter would upset your mother."

Grace took a deep breath and said quietly, "Then I guess, as my mother always told me, I must make do."

But Nancy could see the pain in Grace's eyes. She shook her head, insisting, "Somehow we will find a way to get that letter to your mother, Grace. When she sees it, she'll be very proud of you."

Grace softly said, "My mother always has been proud of me."

It was hard for Nancy to speak, but she managed to say, "I am proud of you, too."

"I thank you, Mistress Nancy," Grace whispered.

Voices were coming from the bedchamber, so Nancy hurried to join her father and Elizabeth.

Elizabeth lay in bed propped on a stack of feather pillows. Her face was blotchy and her eyelids swollen with tears.

"Poor Elizabeth. Poor Elizabeth," Mr. Geddy said. He patted her hand clumsily.

"I'm sorry," Elizabeth said. She looked from her husband to Nancy. "I wanted to decorate the house for the Christmas season, so it would be festive for you when you returned. It was little enough to do, and I did it badly. Now I've called you away from the only holiday festivities you were to have."

Nancy, moved by Elizabeth's efforts and filled with care and concern for her, perched on the side of Elizabeth's bed. Wrapping her arms around Elizabeth's shoulders, she said, "Thank you for trying to make the house beautiful for us."

She sat up and smiled at Elizabeth. "Now it's my turn. I'll make the house beautiful for *you*. I'll take such good care of you that you needn't lift a finger. And I'll bake you a pudding as smooth as silk. We'll celebrate the twelve days of Christmas in our own way."

Nancy took a deep breath, and her smile deepened. "And when your ankle has healed, I hope that you'll teach me to make your mother's queen's cake."

Elizabeth smiled in return. "It will be my great pleasure," she said.

As Nancy recognized the shy hope in Elizabeth's eyes she realized that the ball didn't matter. Dancing with Charles Pelham didn't matter. He might have been very handsome, but he was far too old for her anyway. What mattered was doing what she could to make Papa and Elizabeth happy . . . and bring all of them together as a family.

Nancy bent to kiss Elizabeth's cheek. "Thank you, Mama," she said.

Epilogue

"Well?" Lori asked as Mrs. Otts finished her story. "What about Elizabeth's baby? Tell us what happened."

Mrs. Otts chuckled. "Ah, the baby was a fine, healthy girl, born April sixteenth, 1766. She was named Mary Geddy but called Polly. She was but the second of Nancy's four half sisters and half brothers, and I'm sure Nancy treasured each and every one of them."

Stewart shrugged. "I've heard enough about babies. What happened with the Stamp Act? How long did it take the king to repeal it?"

"On March eighteenth, 1766, King George III signed the repeal of the Stamp Act," Mrs. Otts said.

"However, at the same time, he signed the Declaratory Act, which denied that the colonists were exempt from parliamentary taxes or law."

Chip frowned. "So there was still taxation without representation."

"The colonists did remain loyal to the Crown. For the most part they were pleased to have the Stamp Act repealed and life returned to what they considered to be normal."

Lori sighed. "I'm sorry Nancy didn't get a chance to dance with Charles Pelham. Did she date him later, when she was older?"

"No, I'm afraid not," Mrs. Otts said. The Pelham family, however, led a very unusual life. The older two brothers, Peter junior and Charles, had already left home in 1771, when Peter Pelham took a second job. His position as the Bruton Parish Church organist didn't pay enough to support his many children, so he applied for the job of gaoler and won the appointment."

She slowly shook her head as she added, "That meant he and his family had to live in rooms within the building that held the gaol. 'Twas most hard on his son, Will. To get to his bedchamber at night Will had to pass the cells holding criminals who were headed for the whip or even for hanging. He tried scurrying past in the dark, not looking in their direction, even though he could hear the rattle of the chains attached to a prisoner's leg and an occasional moan or cough from a prisoner who was sleeping badly.

"Then one night an accused horse thief named Jake hissed through the bars at Will, 'Come closer. I have something important to tell you.'

"Against his better judgment, Will listened, and what he heard caused chills to shoot up his backbone. According to Jake, the ghost of the pirate Blackbeard, furious that some of his crew had been held in the gaol before they were sentenced to be hanged, was haunting the gaol and was up to no good."

Chip stared in astonishment. "Will had to live in a jail that was haunted by a pirate ghost? What did he do?"

"He ran into a good bit of trouble, he did," Mrs. Otts said.

"With the ghost?"

"With something even worse."

A woman stepped up to the stall and picked up a cap. "Do you have one with a pink ribbon?" she asked.

"Here you are," Mrs. Otts replied handing her a cap.

Turning back to Chip, she said, "If you and your friends come back later, when the stalls are closing, I'll have time to tell you Will Pelham's story. I know you'll find it quite exciting."

Author's Note

The year 1765 was politically important in Williamsburg, Virginia, because in that year the Stamp Act was imposed upon all the colonists in America. The refusal of the colonists to accept the Stamp Act became one very important step toward their eventual fight for independence.

I knew I would be writing about Anne Geddy, called Nancy, who was twelve years old in 1765, and in my story I wanted to show how the Stamp Act affected Nancy, her silversmith father, and the community of Williamsburg. Yet when I read through the Colonial Williamsburg Foundation's resource material, searching for the information I needed to develop Nancy's story and write this book, another important aspect of Nancy's life began to stand out.

In the 1700s, with none of the modern medications we have on hand today, many illnesses caused deaths. It was common for men and women to remarry if their first—or even second or third—partner died.

Only a very few women were able to work to support themselves, so widows who needed the financial security of a husband soon remarried. So did widowers, who depended upon wives to run their households and raise their children. This meant that many children grew up in mixed families, with half sisters and half brothers and stepbrothers and stepsisters.

Were all these family joinings happy? Peaceful? I don't think so. There were bound to have been personality conflicts.

When I read all the available information about the Geddy family, I discovered that Colonial Williamsburg historians believe that Elizabeth Waddill was the second wife of James Geddy, Jr., and was not Nancy's mother. They do not know who Nancy's mother was or when she died.

What if James's first wife had died soon after the birth of their daughter, Nancy, and he had waited a long ten years to remarry? Surely Nancy would have resented the sudden appearance of a stepmother, who would immediately take charge of the household.

What if Nancy greatly missed and idolized the joyful, loving, happy Elizabeth—the mother she knew only through tales her father and grandmother told her?

What if her stepmother, unfortunately also named Elizabeth, was painfully shy and so ill at ease with Nancy that she came across as stern and unloving?

What if the conflict between Nancy and her stepmother kept growing and became too much for Nancy to handle?

I needed to understand Nancy, so my first step was to determine what her personality might have been. I think she was used to thinking she was in charge. She was well aware of her father's admonitions that a young lady does not "put herself forward," but I guessed that she must have strongly felt that if something needed to be done, she should *do* it. I knew that in my story Nancy was going to cause problems for herself, but I was positive that Nancy was also going to solve problems.

The Colonial Williamsburg Foundation's records show that Nancy's half brothers were James

Geddy III, who was born around 1764, and William Waddill Geddy, who was born about 1768. Her half sisters were Mary (Polly) Geddy, born in 1766, and Elizabeth (Betsey) Geddy, born around 1770.

When Nancy was about nineteen, in March 1772, she married John Brown, a clerk in the secretary of Virginia's office. She eventually moved with her husband to Richmond. They had three daughters, Judith, Nancy, and Maria.

James Geddy, Jr., served on Williamsburg's Common Council in 1767. Although he took an active part in the town's public life, he may have been a reluctant patriot. He apparently did not sign the 1769 nonimportation agreement. In July 1770, however, Geddy signed a new nonimportation agreement. He showed public support for the patriot cause again in 1775, when he served on the Committee of Safety.

When I read an interpreter's biography about a slave named Nanny, I realized what James Geddy, Jr., must have been like.

Nanny and her daughter, Sukey, belonged to Lieutenant Governor Francis Fauquier. The lieutenant governor disliked being a slave owner and provided in his will, when he died in 1768, that his slaves "have the liberty to choose their own Master and that the Women and their Children shall not be parted."

Nanny chose James Geddy, Jr., as her new master. Perhaps she selected him because he was known as a kind, fair, and considerate man. Geddy readily agreed to buy Nanny and Sukey from Fauquier's estate, even though they were valued at sixty-five British pounds.

The Benjamin Powell family's business and land holdings prospered. Powell was also active as a public servant for Williamsburg and York County.

Hannah grew up to marry William Drew, clerk of Berkeley County (now in West Virginia), and named her son Benjamin, after her father. Her sister, Ann, married John Burwell of Williamsburg.

We do not know why Henry "Harry" Armistead remained with his grandparents and did not return to his home after his father's death. We do know, however, that Harry was a great favorite with his stepgrandfather, Henry Wetherburn. When Wetherburn died he left Harry a silver watch, a personal slave named Dick, and enough money for Harry's education at William and Mary, beginning with the college's grammar school. Harry probably boarded at the school, his slave with him, and may have spent the time between terms with his grandmother.

We don't know the future of apprentice Tom Dugar, but we can assume he learned his skills well and went into his adult life as a well-paid journeyman tradesman.

The colonists' bravery in protesting the Stamp Act paid off when King George repealed the Stamp Act on March 18, 1766. Today we've become so used to news on the spot, it's hard to realize that it wasn't until May 2, 1766, that news of the repeal of the Stamp Act was first published in the *Virginia Gazette.*

I enjoyed writing about the hated Stamp Act from Nancy Geddy's point of view and imagining what she might have done in order to influence her father. It's not just adults who play a part in creating history. Children do, too.

About Williamsburg

The story of Williamsburg, the capital of eighteenth-century Virginia, began more than seventy-five years before the thirteen original colonies became the United States in 1776.

Williamsburg was the colony's second capital. Jamestown, the first permanent English settlement in North America, was the first. Jamestown stood on a swampy peninsula in the James River, and over the years, people found it an unhealthy place to live. They also feared that ships sailing up the river could attack the town.

In 1699, a year after the Statehouse at Jamestown burned down for the fourth time, Virginians decided to move the capital a few miles away, to a place known as

The Capitol at Williamsburg

Middle Plantation. On high ground between two rivers, Middle Plantation was a healthier and safer location that was already home to several of Virginia's leading citizens.

Middle Plantation was also the home of the College of William and Mary, today one of Virginia's most revered institutions. The College received its charter from King William III and Queen Mary II of England in 1693. Its graduates include two of our nation's first presidents: Thomas Jefferson and James Monroe.

The new capital's name was changed to Williamsburg in honor of King William. Like the Virginia colony, Williamsburg grew during the eighteenth century. Government officials and their families arrived. Taverns opened for business, and merchants and artisans settled in. Much of the heavy labor and domestic work was performed by African Americans, most of them slaves, although a few were free. By the eve of the American Revolution, nearly two thousand people—roughly half of them white and half of them black—lived in Williamsburg.

The Revolutionary War and Its Leaders

The formal dates of the American Revolution are 1775 to 1783, but the problems between the thirteen original colonies and Great Britain, their mother country, began in 1765, when Parliament enacted the Stamp Act.

England was in debt from fighting the Seven Years War (called the French and Indian War in the colonies) and believed that the colonists should help pay the debt. The colonists were stunned. They considered themselves English and believed that they had the same political rights as people living in

England. These rights included being taxed *only* by an elected body, such as each colony's legislature. Now a body in which they were not represented, Parliament, was taxing them.

All thirteen colonies protested, and the Stamp Act was repealed in 1766. Over the next nine years, however, Great Britain imposed other taxes and enacted other laws that the colonists believed infringed on their rights. Finally, in 1775, the Second Continental Congress, made up of representatives from twelve of the colonies, established an army. The following year, the Congress (now with representatives from all

A reenactment of Virginia legislators debating the Stamp Act

thirteen colonies) declared independence from Great Britain.

The Revolutionary War was the historical event that ensured Williamsburg's place in American history. Events that happened there and the people who participated in them helped form the values on which the United States was founded. Virginians meeting in Williamsburg helped lead the thirteen colonies to independence.

In fact, Americans first declared independence in the Capitol building in Williamsburg. There, on May 15, 1776, the colony's leaders declared Virginia's full freedom from England. In a unanimous vote, they also instructed the colony's representatives to the Continental Congress to propose that the Congress "declare the United Colonies free and independent states absolved from all allegiances to or dependence upon the Crown or Parliament of Great Britain."

Three weeks later, Richard Henry Lee, one of Virginia's delegates, stood before the Congress and proposed independence. His action led directly to the writing of the Declaration of Independence. The Congress adopted the Declaration on July 2 and signed it two days later. The United States of America was born.

Williamsburg served as a training ground for

three noteworthy patriots: George Washington, Thomas Jefferson, and Patrick Henry. Each arrived in Williamsburg as a young man, and there each matured into a statesman.

In 1752, George Washington, who later led the American forces to victory over the British in the Revolutionary War and became our nation's first president, came to Williamsburg at the age of nineteen. He soon began a career in the military, which led to a seat in Virginia's legislature, the House of Burgesses. He served as a burgess for sixteen years—negotiating legislation, engaging in political discussions, and building social and political relationships. These experiences helped mold him into one of America's finest political leaders.

Patrick Henry, who would go on to become the first governor of the Commonwealth of Virginia as well as a powerful advocate for the Bill of Rights, first traveled to Williamsburg in 1760 to obtain a law license. Only twenty-three years old, he barely squeaked through the exam. Five years later, as a first-time burgess, he led Virginia's opposition to the Stamp Act. For the next eleven years, Henry's talent as a speaker—including his now famous Caesar-Brutus speech and the immortal cry, "Give me liberty or give me death!"—rallied Virginians to the patriot cause.

Thomas Jefferson, who later wrote the Declaration of Independence, succeeded Patrick Henry as the governor of Virginia, and became the third president of the United States, arrived in Williamsburg in 1760 at the age of seventeen to attend the College of William and Mary. As the cousin of Peyton Randolph, the respected Speaker of the House of Burgesses, Jefferson was immediately welcomed by Williamsburg society. He became a lawyer and was elected a burgess in 1769. In his very first session, the royal governor closed the legislature because it had protested the Townshend Acts. The burgesses moved the meeting to the Raleigh Tavern, where they drew up an agreement to boycott British goods.

Jefferson, Henry, and Washington each signed the agreement. In the years that followed, all three men supported the patriot cause and the nation that grew out of it.

Williamsburg Then and Now

Williamsburg in the eighteenth century was a vibrant American town. Thanks largely to the vision of the Reverend Dr. W. A. R. Goodwin, rector of Bruton Parish Church at the opening of the twentieth cen-

The Reverend Dr. W.A.R. Goodwin with John D. Rockefeller, Jr.

tury, its vitality can still be experienced today. The generosity of philanthropist John D. Rockefeller, Jr., made it possible to restore Williamsburg to its eighteenth-century glory. Original colonial buildings were acquired and carefully returned to their eighteenth-century appearance. Later houses and buildings were torn down and replaced by carefully researched reconstructions, most built on original eighteenth-century foundations. Rockefeller gave the project both money and enthusiastic support for more than thirty years.

Today, the Historic Area of Williamsburg is both a museum and a living city. The restored buildings, antique furnishings, and costumed interpreters can help you create a picture of the past in your mind's eye. The Historic Area is operated by the Colonial Williamsburg Foundation, a nonprofit educational organization staffed by historians, interpreters, actors, administrators, numerous people behind the scenes, and many volunteers. They invite you to visit their fair city and conjure up the life and times of our colonial forebears in your imagination.

Williamsburg is a living reminder of our country's past and a guide to its future; it shows us where we have been and can give us clues about where we may be going. Though the stories of the people who lived in eighteenth-century Williamsburg may seem very different from our lives in the twenty-first century, the heart of the stories remains the same. We created a nation based on new ideas about liberty, independence, and democracy. The Colonial Williamsburg: Young Americans books are about individuals who may not have experienced these principles in their own lives, but whose lives foreshadowed changes for the generations that followed. People like the smart and capable Ann McKenzie of *Ann's Story: 1747*, who struggled to reconcile her interest in medicine with

A scene from Colonial Williamsburg today

society's expectations for an eighteenth-century woman. People like the brave Caesar of *Caesar's Story: 1759,* who struggled in silence against the institution of slavery that gripped his people, his family, and himself. While some of these lives evoke painful memories in our country's history, they are a part of that history nonetheless and cannot be forgotten. These stories form the foundation of our country. The people in them are the unspoken heroes of our time.

Childhood in Eighteenth-Century Virginia

If you traveled back in time to Virginia in the 1700s, some things would probably seem familiar to you. Colonial children played some of the same games that children play today: blindman's buff, hopscotch, leapfrog, and hide-and-seek. Girls had dolls, boys flew kites, and both boys and girls might play with puzzles and read.

You might be surprised, however, at how few toys even well-to-do children owned. Adults and children in the 1700s owned far fewer things than we do today, not only fewer toys but also less furniture and clothing. And the books children read were either educational or taught them how to behave properly, such as *Aesop's Fables* and the *School of Manners.*

Small children dressed almost alike back then. Boys and girls in prosperous families wore gowns

(dresses) similar to the ones older girls and women wore. Less well-to-do white children and enslaved children wore shifts, which were much like our nightgowns. Both black and white boys began wearing pants when they were between five and seven years old.

Boys and girls in Colonial Virginia began doing chores when they were six or seven, probably the same age at which *you* started doing chores around the house. But their chores included tasks such as toting kindling, grinding corn with a mortar and pestle, and turning a spit so that meat would roast evenly over the fire.

These chores were done by both black and white children. Many enslaved children began working in the fields at this age. They might pick worms off tobacco, carry water to older workers, hoe, or pull weeds. However, they usually were not expected to do as much work as the adults.

As black and white children grew older, they were assigned more and sometimes harder chores. Few children of either race went to school. Those who did usually came from prosperous white families, although there were some charity schools. Some middling (middle-class) and gentry (upper-class) children studied at home with tutors. Other white children learned from their mothers and fathers to read, write, and do simple arithmetic. But not all white children were taught these skills, and very few enslaved children learned them.

When they were ten, eleven, or twelve years old, children began preparing in earnest for adulthood.

Boys from well-to-do families got a university education at the College of William and Mary in Williamsburg
or at a university in England. Their advanced studies
prepared them to manage the plantations they inherited
or to become lawyers and important government officials. Many did all three things.

Many middle-class boys and some poorer ones became apprentices. An apprentice agreed to work for a master for several years, usually until the apprentice turned twenty-one. The master agreed to teach the apprentice his trade or profession, to ensure that he learned to read and write, and, usually, to feed, clothe,

An apprentice with the master cabinetmaker

and house him. Apprentices became apothecaries (druggist-doctors), blacksmiths, carpenters, coopers (barrel makers), founders (men who cast metals in a foundry), merchants, printers, shoemakers, silversmiths, store clerks, and wigmakers. Some girls, usually orphans with no families, also became apprentices. A girl apprentice usually lived with a family and worked as a domestic servant.

Most white girls, however, learned at home. Their mothers or other female relatives taught them the skills they would need to manage their households after they married—such as cooking, sewing, knitting, cleaning, doing the laundry, managing domestic slaves, and caring for ailing family members. Some middle-class and most gentry girls also learned music, dance, embroidery, and sometimes French. Formal education for girls of all classes, however, was usually limited to reading, writing, and arithmetic.

Enslaved children also began training for adulthood when they were ten to twelve years old. Some boys and girls worked in the house and learned to be domestic slaves. Others worked in the fields. Some boys learned a trade.

Because masters had to pay taxes on slaves who were sixteen or older, slaves were expected to do a full day's work when they turned sixteen, if not sooner. White boys, however, usually were not considered adults until they reached the age of twenty-one. White girls were considered adults when they turned twenty-one or married, whichever came first.

Enslaved or free black boys watching tradesmen saw wood

When we look back, we see many elements of colonial childhood that are familiar to us—the love of toys and games, the need to help the family around the house, and the task of preparing for adulthood. However, it is interesting to compare the days of a colonial child to the days of a child today, and to see all the ways in which life has changed for children over the years.

The Stamp Act

In 1763 Great Britain defeated the French in the Seven Years War (known in America as the French and Indian War). However, Britain had large financial problems because of debt from the war and the cost of stationing an army in the colonies to defend its new land.

The British government thought the American colonies ought to help pay for the army that would protect them. In 1764 Parliament first discussed the idea of a stamp tax to raise money from the colonists.

Taxes in the colonies weren't new. The colonists were used to paying taxes passed by their own legislatures. As Nancy's father explained to her, the colonists did not have a representative in Parliament. When the colonists heard that Parliament might tax them, many began to protest because they believed that only their elected representatives should tax them.

Colonial legislatures sent petitions to Parliament to protest the new tax. Their efforts were wasted. The Stamp Act became law on March 22, 1765.

The Stamp Act taxed mainly documents, which had to be written or printed on specially stamped paper. These included court documents, the papers needed by ships to leave a colonial harbor, land grants and deeds, apprenticeship agreements, news-

Virginia's legislators debate the colony's stand on the Stamp Act.

papers, and newspaper advertisements. Even playing cards and dice were taxed.

Nancy knew that the Stamp Act might hurt her family's business. Taxing court documents could make it too expensive for her family to use the courts to collect the debts their customers owed them. Also, Virginians were already paying high taxes, and the price of tobacco, their staple crop, had fallen. If customers had less money to spend, they probably wouldn't buy luxury items like silver. With less

A protest against the Stamp Act appears on this creamware teapot from 1765.

money and less work to do, Nancy's uncle might have had to dismiss Tom, his apprentice.

Nancy was not the only colonist who worried about the effects of the Stamp Act. Virginia and the other colonies continued to protest the act after it had been passed. Virginia and other colonial legislators wrote declarations against the tax that were printed in other colonies' newspapers.

The colonists also pressured the appointed agents to resign before the Stamp Act took effect November 1, 1765. In some colonies, such as Massachusetts and Maryland, mobs became violent and destroyed

An angry crowd confronts Virginia's Stamp Act agent, George Mercer, and convinces him to resign.

the homes of agents. In Williamsburg, the angry crowd in which Nancy found herself persuaded Virginia's agent, George Mercer, to resign. Tension over the act eased for a time.

The protests eventually worked. On March 18, 1766, King George III signed the repeal of the Stamp Act. Virginians celebrated with a ball at the Capitol and drank toasts to the king. They paid little attention to the Declaratory Act, which the king signed on the same day as the repeal.

The Declaratory Act stated that Parliament had authority over the colonies and that the colonists were not exempt from taxes or laws passed by Parliament. The conflict between Britain and its American colonies had not been resolved after all. In fact, the struggle was just beginning. Only the American Revolution would resolve the issue of American rights.

Recipe for Lemon Tarts

(12 small tarts)

Nancy Geddy baked lemon tarts during the cooking lesson with Mrs. Powell and her daughters, Hannah and Ann. She also made this treat for the tea she prepared so that her father could discuss politics with Mr. Powell and Mr. Greenhow. With help from an adult, you can make the same lemon tarts using the recipe below.

    1³/₄ cups sugar
    juice of 2 lemons (6 to 8 tablespoons)
    rind of 2 lemons, grated
    ¹/₂ cup butter
    6 eggs, well beaten
    12 frozen tart shells, baked according to the
        directions on the package

Mix the sugar, juice, and rind.

Melt the butter in the top of a double boiler. Add the sugar mixture and eggs.

Continue cooking over hot water until very thick, stirring constantly.

Cool, cover, and refrigerate.

When the filling is chilled, fill the tart shells.

About the
Author

Joan Lowery Nixon is the acclaimed author of more than a hundred books for young readers. She has served as president of the Mystery Writers of America and as regional vice president for the Southwest Chapter of that society. She is the only four-time winner of the Edgar Allan Poe Best Juvenile Mystery Award, given by the Mystery Writers of America, and is also a two-time winner of the Golden Spur Award for best juvenile Western, for two of the novels in her Orphan Train Adventures series.

Joan Lowery Nixon and her husband live in Houston.